The Strange Cabin on Catamount Island

Lawrence J. Leslie

"THE VOYAGE WAS RESUMED"

CONTENTS

CHAPTER I.

HOW THE DARE WAS GIVEN.

"And so Herb Benson dared you, Max, you say?"

"That's what he did, Steve."

"To camp on Catamount Island?"

"And stay there a full week. He said that even if we did have nerve enough to make the *try*, he'd give us just one solitary night to hang out there!"

"Huh! just because Herb and his old club got scared nearly to death a while ago by some silly noise they thought was a ghost, they reckon every fellow is built on the same plan, don't they, Max?"

"I guess that's what they do, Steve."

"So they challenge us to make a camp, and stick it out, do they? What did you tell Herb? Oh, I hope you just took him up on the spot!"

"Well, I said I'd put it up to the rest of the chums, my cousin, Owen Hastings, Toby Jucklin, Bandy-legs Griffin, and yourself."

"Count me in as ready to accept the dare. Why, I'd start this blessed minute if I had my way, Max!"

"I know you would, because you're always so quick to flare up. That's why they all call you 'Touch-and-go Steve Dowdy.' But come along, and let's get the other fellows. We can go down to the boathouse and talk it over, anyhow."

"But tell me first, when *can* we be ready to go, Max—some time to-morrow?"

1

"You certainly are the most impatient fellow I ever knew," replied Max, with a laugh; "yes, if the other boys are willing, I guess we might get off at noon to-morrow. It wouldn't take long to lay in our supplies; and you know we've already got tents, cooking things, and all that stuff on hand."

"Oh, shucks! leave the grub part of the business to me," remarked Steve, instantly. "What's the use of having a chum whose daddy is the leading grocer in Carson if he can't look after the supplies. But I'm just tickled nearly to death at the chance of this little cruise up the Big Sunflower."

"I can guess why," Max observed, as he kept pace with his nervous companion's quick strides.

"The new canoes!" exclaimed Steve; "it gives us the chance we've been wanting to find out how they work in real harness. We've only tried little spins in them so far, you know, Max. Gee! I hated like everything to let my motorcycle go; but the folks put their foot down hard, after that second accident to our chum, Bandy-legs; and, like the rest of the bunch, I had to send it back to the shop for what it was worth. It was like going to the scrapheap with it, because I lost so much money."

"Well, let's hope we can make it up in fun on the water with our boats," was the sensible way the other put it. "Here's Ordway's drug store, and we can use his 'phone to get the rest of the crowd along."

A minute later, and inside the booth they were calling for M-23 West. It was not later than eight-twenty in the evening when the two boys met down in front of the hardware store, where a brilliant light burned all night long; so that the evening was young when Max caught the well-known voice of Toby Jucklin at the other end of the wire.

Toby stuttered, at times, fearfully. He kept trying to overcome the habit, and the result was that his affliction came and went in spasms. Sometimes he could talk as well as any one of his four chums; then

2

again, especially when excited, he would have a serious lapse, being compelled to resort to his old trick of giving a sharp whistle, and then stopping a couple of seconds to get a grasp on himself, when he was able to say what he wanted intelligently.

"That you, Max?" asked Toby, who had lived with an old, crabbed uncle and been treated harshly, despite the fact that his father had left quite a little fortune for him when of age; until Mr. Hastings took hold of the case, had the court depose Uncle Ambrose, and place the boy in charge of a generous gentleman whose name was Mr. Jackson, with whom he now lived in comfort.

"Just who it is, Toby," replied the other. "Say, can't you hike down to the boathouse and meet us there?"

"Now?" demanded Toby, his voice beginning to show signs of wabbling.

"As soon as you can get there," was what Max answered.

"Hey! what's on the carpet now, tell me, Max?" demanded Toby, quickly.

"Keep cool," warned the boy in the booth. "Steve is here with me in the drug store. We've got a scheme for a little outing in our canoes, and want to put it up to the rest of the bunch. How about coming down, Toby?"

"S-s-sure I'll b-b-be there!" exclaimed the other.

"Then make a start soon," and with that Max rang off, because he knew Toby would hold him indefinitely if once he got started asking questions and stuttering at the same time.

He soon had another boy on the wire, this time Bandy-legs. And the response was as rapid and favorable in this quarter as it had been with Toby. From the tone of the inquiries Max made, the boys understood there must be something out of the common on tap, and their curiosity was therefore excited. They would have been at the place of meeting, even though they found it necessary to crawl out of bedroom windows and slide down the post of the front porch; which in neither case was required, for both Toby and the other chum had plenty of freedom.

When Owen, who, being an orphan, lived at his cousin's house, had been brought to the 'phone and asked to join the rest for a serious consultation, Max "shut up shop," as he called it.

"Let's get a move on ourselves now, Steve," he remarked, as they left the booth, "and hustle around to the little boathouse my splendid dad bought for us when we got the canoes. It isn't a beauty, but it answers our purpose fine."

"Just what it does," replied Steve, as they walked out of the store. "I reckon all the boys are on their way by now, eh, Max?"

"I'd like to see anything hold them back after the way I stirred things up. Why, just as like as not even poor old Bandy-legs is tumbling all over himself, sprinting down to the river through the dark."

"He does have the greatest time trying to keep his legs from tripping him up," remarked Steve; "but all the same there never was a better chum going than Bandy-legs Griffin. In a pinch he'd stand by you to the limit, no matter what happened. But hurry, Max; as we did the calling, it's up to us to get there ahead of the rest, and have the lamps lit. Wow! I barked my shin then to beat the band. Hang the dark, say I!"

"A little slower, Steve," cautioned the other, catching hold of his chum's coat sleeve. "Rome wasn't built in a day, you know. We'll get there just as soon, and with our skin whole, if only you don't rush things so hard."

"I can see the boathouse ahead there, I think," suggested Steve, presently.

"That's right; and we're the first after all, you see, because every fellow has a key, and if any one got in ahead of us we'd notice a light in the window. Hello! who's that?"

"Think you saw something, did you, Max?" asked the other; "but as there wasn't any answer, I guess you must have been off your base that time."

"Perhaps I was," replied the other; "but here we are at the door now, and as I've got my key handy, I'll open up."

The boathouse had once been some sort of low, squatty building, which, being made over, answered the new purpose very well. And when Max had started a couple of lamps to burning the prospect was cheery enough. Several canoes were ranged in racks along one side. Three of these were single canoes; the other a larger boat, which two of the boys paddled, and they called it the war canoe.

Hardly had they reached this point than there was heard the sound of a voice at the door. Steve opened it to admit a panting boy, whose short lower extremities had a positive inclination to pattern a little after the type of bows, which gave Bandy-legs the name by which he was known far and wide.

Then came Owen Hastings, a quiet sort of a fellow, looking very like his cousin Max; and a minute later Toby Jucklin appeared.

"Now open up, and explain what all this fuss and feathers means?" demanded Owen, as the five gathered around the table upon which the larger lamp stood.

The boys expected to fit this building up as a sort of club room later on, and in this place during the next winter keep all their magazines, as well as other treasures connected with their association, together.

So Max explained just how it came that Herb Benson, the leader of another group of Carson boys, had challenged them to spend a certain length of time on Catamount Island, far up the Big Sunflower branch of the Evergreen River, which flowed past the town.

Some time previous to this Max and his four chums, wishing to secure funds in order to carry out certain pet projects for the summer vacation, and early fall, had conceived the notion that perhaps the mussels, or fresh-water clams, that could be found, particularly along the Big Sunflower, might contain a few pearls such as were being discovered in so many streams in Indiana, Arkansas, and other Middle Western States.

They had been fairly successful, and during a search discovered a number of really valuable pearls. From the proceeds of the sale of a portion of their find they had purchased motorcycles, with which they enjoyed a few runs. Then, as Steve had remarked so forlornly, Bandy-legs being so clumsy with his mount as to have a few accidents, which, however, had not been serious, their folks had united in declaring war on the gas-engine business. Consequently they had been compelled to dispose of the machines at a sacrifice. And the canoes had been their second choice.

After the other three had heard what the proposal was, they united in declaring their perfect willingness to take up the dare, if only to show Herb that there was a big difference between his brand of nerve, and that which the five chums possessed.

Of the lot possibly Bandy-legs was the only one who did not show great enthusiasm over the project. Max noticed that he seemed to simply let the others do the talking, though when a vote was taken upon whether or not they should accept the challenge, the Griffin boy's hand went up with the rest. Still, that was certainly a sigh that broke from his lips.

"What's the matter, Bandy-legs? Don't you feel like making the try?" demanded the impetuous Steve, quick to notice that the other was not brimming over with the same kind of eagerness that actuated himself.

"Oh! I'm going along, all right," declared the shorter chum, doggedly. "Ketch me staying out when the rest of you want to go. But I never dreamed I'd ever pluck up the nerve to stay a night on that blooming island. Why, ever since I c'n remember I've heard the tallest yarns about it. Some say it's just a nest of crawlers; and others, that all the varmints left unshot in the big timber up beyond have a roost on that strip of land in the middle of the river."

"Rats!" scoffed Steve, derisively. "That's all talk; hot air, you might say. Don't believe there's any truth in it, any more'n that story about ghosts, and queer noises that Herb and his crowd tell about. Anyhow, I never let a dare go past me."

"That's right, Steve," remarked Owen; "it acts on you just like a red flag does on a bull. But it's decided, is it, fellows, that we go to-morrow noon?"

"We ought to be able to paddle up there in five hours or so," remarked Max.

"Sure, and I'm in fine trim for the job; how about you, Toby?" Owen continued, for the stuttering boy was to be his mate in the double canoe, which could hold the tents, and some of the more cumbrous luggage devoted to camping comfort.

"Just aching for exercise," the other managed to say, promptly enough.

"Well, I reckon we'll all get what we want," Max remarked, as they prepared to quit the boathouse; "for the current is pretty strong in places, and the island lies a good many miles off. Everybody be on hand early to-morrow, for we've got a heap of things to do before lunch time. Skip out now; I'm going to douse the glim."

As the chattering boys walked away in the darkness they were followed by a stealthy figure that seemed desirous of not being seen. And a little later, when passing a house where a light gleamed from a window, this figure came for just a second in the shaft of light; so

7

that had any one of the five chums happened to glance behind just then they might have recognized the evil face of their most vindictive enemy, Ted Shafter, the bully of Carson!

CHAPTER II.

BANDY-LEGS IN TROUBLE.

At noon on the following day there was more or less excitement around the spot where the boathouse stood. The canoes, already loaded, lay moored near by, awaiting the word to be given that would send the little expedition on its way up-stream.

Of course the news had got abroad, though Max would much rather have kept it a secret, if they could. But Herb and his friends, as well as some other boys of the river town, were on hand to see the start.

And as was natural, a heap of good-natured chaffing was indulged in. All sorts of dismal predictions were made by Herb, and those of his comrades who had been in his company at the time of their wild midnight flight from Catamount Island.

"We'll expect to see you to-morrow, all right, fellows!" cried one.

"Yes, and we're going to keep tabs on you, if you don't show up," remarked still another. "It won't be fair to sleep on the mainland, and just go over in the day. You've got to stay right there a whole week, night after night, to win out. See?"

"A week," answered Steve, laughing in a scoffing manner; "why, if it wasn't a waste of good time, we'd have made it a month. But we've got other fish to fry, and don't want to spend all our vacation on that measly old island."

"Yes, say what you like," called Herb, as the canoes began to leave the shore, and the paddles to flash in the noonday sun's bright rays; "you'll have another story to tell when you show up to-morrow, or I miss my guess."

"Wait till you see that old cabin, that's what!" called out another, in a mysterious way that somehow caused Bandy-legs to look uneasy, Max thought.

He knew that if there was going to be a weak link in the chain it would lie in that quarter; for the short chum had a few silly notions concerning certain things, and was not wholly free from a belief in supernatural happenings. But with the backing of four sturdy chums, Bandy-legs ought to brace up, and show himself a true boy of nerve.

"Look at that Shack Beggs making faces after us!" remarked Steve, who, as usual, threatened to take the lead in the push up the Evergreen current.

"I noticed him hangin' around all the time," added Bandy-legs; "and every now and then he'd seem to grin, and shake hands with himself, like he felt nearly too good to keep the thing quiet. Whatever ails him, d'ye think, Max?"

"Well, as I never stood for a mind reader, I can't tell you," was the reply of the one addressed; "but as we know he belongs to that Ted Shafter crowd, it's easy to understand that he just believes something terrible is going to happen to us up on Catamount Island."

"Oh! I hope he's barking up the wrong tree, then!" exclaimed Bandy-legs.

"Just what he's doing, take my word for it," Owen put in, from the stern of the big war canoe, which he and Toby were urging against the flowing current with lusty strokes, and evident keen enjoyment.

"How does it go?" asked Max, who was in a sixteen-foot canvas canoe like the one Steve handled so dexterously; while Bandy-legs, fearing to trust to anything so frail, had insisted on getting one of the older type lapstreak cedar boats, that were so marvelously beautiful in his eyes.

"Fine as silk!" announced Steve, from up ahead.

"Ditto here!" echoed Toby, and Owen added his words of praise.

"It seems like bully good fun!" declared Bandy-legs, who was puffing a little, his boat being somewhat more weighty than the other two single canoes, and who consequently was somewhat behind the rest; "but I wish you'd get a rope on Steve there, and hold him in. He ain't fit to be the pace-maker. I just *can't* keep going like wildfire all the time."

"That's right, too" remarked Max. "We ought to let up a little in the start. It never is good policy to do your best in the beginning of a race. And we've really got loads of time to make that island before nightfall."

Of course Steve could do as he pleased; but since the others dropped back a little so as to accommodate the less skillful Bandy-legs, he had to follow suit, or be all alone in the van. Steve grumbled more or less because some fellows never could "get a move on 'em," as he complained; but outside of making an occasional little spurt, and then resting, he stuck pretty well by his mates during the next hour or two.

Then something happened, something that they had never once dreamed of, and which was at first utterly beyond the understanding of any of the paddlers.

Bandy-legs seemed to find more or less trouble about getting himself settled in the best attitude for his work. It was all pretty new for him, though Max thought the other did very well for a greenhorn. He wriggled about in his cedar boat like an uneasy worm, changing his position often, and each time thinking that he had improved his paddling powers, only to find the same old fault.

All at once he set up a whoop that startled his chums.

"Hi! looky here, what's happenin' to this old coffin!"

The others saw nothing wrong, save that Bandy-legs himself seemed to be engaged in scrambling about more or less, as though he had suddenly discovered a venomous spider crawling out from under the false bottom of his delicate craft.

"What ails you?" called out Max, stopping the use of his handy spruce blade, as he turned his head toward the one who appeared to be in trouble.

"Wow! I tell you she's sinkin'!" continued Bandy-legs, as if aghast.

"What! your canoe?" cried Owen, as if unable to believe his ears.

"Sure she is, boys! Water's just bubbling up in her to beat the band! I felt it gettin' wet down by my feet, and looked just in time. What'll I do—jump over and swim for the shore right here?"

"Don't be silly, Bandy-legs!" cried Max. "If something has happened to your boat, why, head for the shore, and paddle hard. It ain't so far away but you can reach it easy enough. You must have hit a snag, and punched a hole in the skin of the canoe."

"I never hit nothin'!" called back the other, as in his clumsy fashion he managed to presently change the course of his boat, and start for the nearest bank, with the war canoe and that of Max accompanying him.

"Hey, what you goin' to do, have a snack?" yelled Steve, who at that moment chanced to be a little way ahead of the others.

"Bandy-legs is sinking, and we've got to see what ails his boat!" answered Max, making a speaking tube or a megaphone of his hands.

No doubt Steve, impatient to reach their destination, and make camp before dark, would be saying things not at all complimentary to the sufferer, as he retraced his course, in order to join them.

Meanwhile, when the canoes reached a pebbly stretch of shore, they were beached; and then Max set to work to ascertain what could have happened to the cedar boat to make it start sinking in such a mysterious way.

First the bundles were taken out, and they all observed that it was fortunate they had decided at the last minute to let Bandy-legs have one of the tents instead of the foodstuff he had been given in the beginning.

"Give me a hand here, fellows," remarked Max, "and we'll turn her over to let the water get out faster. I can see right now where the trouble lies, and it's right down in the bottom. There's a leak as sure as anything!"

"Then its good-by to my bally little canoe right in the start, I reckon," complained the owner, sadly. "I'm a Jonah, all right. All sorts of things keep happening to *me*. What does it look like, Max?" as the boat was finally turned completely over, so that the bottom was fully exposed.

Max uttered an exclamation that told of astonishment.

"Well, that is queer!" they heard him mutter, as he thrust a finger through the hole in the garboard streak of the boat.

"What strikes you as so funny, Max?" asked Steve, who had by now joined them.

"Look for yourself," replied the other, moving back.

Four heads were instantly bent over, as the boys took his advice.

"Must have been a round snag, all right," commented Steve; "because that's as pretty a circular hole as I ever saw."

"Tell you I never struck no snag!" declared the indignant Bandy-legs; "guess I'd 'a' felt it, wouldn't I, Max?"

"Listen, fellows," said the one appealed to, in a tone that caused the others to stop their wrangling, and pay attention; "as Bandy-legs says, he didn't run foul of any snag on the river since we left home. That hole was made by an auger, or a bit held in a brace. Some mean fellow had the nerve to lay this trap for our chum, in order to give us all the trouble he could."

"Shack Beggs!" shouted Steve, always quick to make up his mind.

"That was why he kept grinning like he did, when he watched us go off," observed Owen, in a disgusted way. "When do you suppose he could have found a chance to do such a dirty trick, Max?"

"Well, we don't know for a certainty whether it was Shack or one of his crowd," replied the other, shaking his head; "but whoever did it must have found some way to get into the boathouse after we left last night. You remember, boys, we've got a ratchet brace there, and several bits. One of them would just about fit this hole. But he must have been mighty careful to take away every little splinter, so as not to make us suspect there'd been any funny carryings-on."

"How d'ye suppose he fixed it, so as to keep the water out till just now?" asked the bewildered owner of the canoe.

For answer Max made a crawl underneath, and almost immediately came out again holding something in his hand, which he showed them. It was apparently a plug of wood, and must have come from the hole that had caused the sudden flooding of the cedar canoe.

"There, you can see what a neat little game he played!" Max exclaimed. After he bored that round hole he made this plug and drove it in from above. Underneath he made sure that it was evened off so it wouldn't be seen unless any one examined the bottom of the canoe close. Then he had it fixed so when Bandy-legs got to moving about, as he always does, you know, any time he was liable to loosen the plug and the pressure of the water'd do the rest.

"Oh! what a wicked shame!" cried the owner of the wrecked canoe.

"H-h-he ought t' b-b-be hung f-f-for it!" exclaimed Toby, just as indignant as though it had been his own boat that was injured so wantonly.

"What can we do, Max, to fix her up?" asked Owen, quietly.

"Oh!" put the plug in again, and make sure that it will hold this time. Later on, when we get back, we'll have to get the boat builder in Carson to put a new streak of cedar planking in, to take the place of this one."

"Sure you can fix it so there won't be any chance of my going down?" asked the anxious owner.

"Easy enough. Just give me ten or fifteen minutes, and I'll answer for it," came the confident response, as Max immediately set to work.

"While this is going on the rest of us can rest," remarked Owen, dropping down on the ground.

"Here's the sandwiches I made this morning; might as well take a bite, now we've got to hang out here a spell," and Bandy-legs began passing them around.

"Looks to me like we had reached the junction of the Big Sunflower and the Elder," observed Steve, as he munched away contentedly at his ham sandwich.

"Just what we have," Max spoke up, working away at his little job, and stopping occasionally to snatch a bite. "It lies right around that bend yonder. I remember it well, and how we made our first haul of the mussels there."

"Yes, and found a bully old pearl in the first lot," declared Steve, watching Bandy-legs poke around in the grass nearby; for the boy with the short legs was of an investigating turn, and liked nothing better than to search for things; "hey! what you think you'll find there, diamonds this time?"

"Oh! I just run across a lot of wriggling little snakes, about as long as lead pencils, and I'm seein' 'em twist and turn. It's just fun to watch the little beggars get mad."

"Huh!" grunted Steve, as he turned his attention to what Max was doing; "some fellers get fun out of mighty little things, sometimes."

A minute or so later they heard Bandy-legs laugh again.

"Say, let up with that silly play, and come in," called Steve, testily; "we're 'bout ready to load up again and go on."

"You'd die laughing to see her try to get a whack at me," called back Bandy-legs. "It's the mother of all them little snakes, I reckon. My! but she's mad though; just coils up here, and jumps out at me every time I touch her with my stick!"

Max felt a shudder pass through his person as he looked at Owen. For suddenly he seemed to realize that the rattling sound, which he had of course thought was caused by a noisy locust on a nearby tree, was in fact the deadly warning that an enraged rattlesnake gives when striving to strike its fangs into an enemy!

CHAPTER III.

ON THE ISLAND WITH THE BAD NAME.

"Keep back, Bandy-legs; that's a rattlesnake!" shouted Max, and some of the others turned white with sudden alarm, as they also noted for the first time the incident buzzing sound from a point nearby.

Immediately every one started toward the spot where the foolish Bandy-legs was standing, holding a rather short stick in his hand, with which he had doubtless been tormenting the larger snake just as he had previously annoyed her young brood.

He was now seemingly turned into stone, although fortunately enough he had managed to spring back a pace upon hearing the dreadful words shouted by his chum.

"Get clubs, and make them as long as you can!" called out Owen. "Be careful how you let her have a chance to reach you when she springs out. A rattlesnake can sometimes strike as far as her own length, they say."

Immediately a scene of great excitement followed. Each fellow ran around, trying to find a suitable stick, that would be stout enough to do execution, and at the same time have sufficient length. For now that they knew what its species was, the coiled serpent looked terribly ugly, as, with head drawn back, she waited for another attack, all the while sounding her rattle like a challenge to battle.

Steve happened to be the first to find a stick that he thought would do the business, and he immediately rushed forward.

"Slow, now, Steve!" warned Max, fearful lest the natural headstrong nature of the other might get him into trouble.

Just then Owen also picked up a long pole, and advanced from the opposite side. The badgered snake, only intent on defending her young, thinking that here was a chance to get away from all this turmoil, had slipped out of coil, and even started to glide off; but as Steve made a wild swoop with his pole, she again flung herself into coil, ready to fight to the end.

Nobody spares a rattlesnake, however much they might wish to let an innocent coachwhip or a common gartersnake get away. From away back to the Garden of Eden times the heel of man has been raised against venomous serpents. And somehow the close call their chum had just had from a terrible danger, seemed to arouse the hostility of the chums against this snake in particular.

When both Max and Toby came up, each, with a part of a hickory limb in their hands, the destiny of that snake was written plainly, strive as she might to escape, or reach one of her human tormentors.

Whack! came Steve's pole down across the reptile's back, and from that instant the fight was taken out of the scaly thing.

"Wow! this is what I call rushing the mourners!" gasped Bandy-legs, after they had made sure that the rattler was as dead as might be expected before sundown; for Owen declared that he had some sort of belief in the old saying that "cut up a snake as you will, its tail will wriggle until sunset."

"I should say yes," added Steve; "and you're bent on bein' in the center of every old thing that happens. First you shout out your boat's sinking, and while we're fixing her you wander out and stir up a hornets' nest about your ears."

"Say, it did sound like it, sure as anything," admitted the repentant Bandy-legs. "I'm sorry I gave you all so much trouble, boys; next time I run across a litter of little snakes, it's me to the woods. Wonder what became of the beggars? They disappeared about the time the mother came tootin' up."

"Mebbe they ran down her throat," suggested Owen; "some say snakes can hide their young that way, but I never believed it."

"Well," remarked Max, who was examining the dead reptile, "this one didn't, so I reckon they must have skedaddled off in the bushes. Perhaps they're old enough to take care of themselves, though I hope they don't live to grow up. If there's one thing I detest on earth it's a poisonous snake."

"Me, too!" piped up Bandy-legs; "but then, you see, I never thought this one was loaded. Yes, I just reckoned she'd come to see what I was doin' with her bunch of youngsters, and I kept on jollyin' her. Thought I was havin' fun, boys, but never again, you hear me!"

"Want to take these rattles along, Bandy-legs?" asked Owen, who had severed the horny looking appendage at the end of the tail; "it'll serve to remind you of what a silly job it is to play with a snake that you've never been properly introduced to."

"Not for me," replied the other, with a little shudder. "I'd just hate to have my folks know how foolish I was. Keep 'em, and hang the thing up in the clubhouse, boys."

"Sure," interrupted Steve; "do for a dinner horn some time; better than Japanese wind bells to make music."

"Ugh! I'll never hear it without thinkin' of the grand scare I got when Max here shouted out the way he did," admitted the one who had been the cause for all this commotion.

"The canoe's ready for business at the old stand," announced Max, "and don't be afraid that there's going to be any trouble again with that same leak. I've fixed that plug in good and strong, Bandy-legs. Now let's be off!"

Accordingly the voyage was resumed. And just as some of the boys had said, they speedily turned from the main river into the branch called the Big Sunflower, which, as the scene of their late successful search for pearls, was invested with memories of a rather pleasant character for the five chums.

As they paddled along against the rather brisk current, first one, and then another had something to call out regarding this place or that.

"It's just great to be coming up here again, after buying these boats with some of the hard cash we earned that time," declared Steve, who was keeping closer to the others now.

"How many fellers d'ye reckon started grubbin' up here, after we quit?" demanded Bandy-legs, who was working the paddle fairly well, though at times he made a bad stroke, and seemed to learn slowly that it could all be done without the splash and noise he insisted on making.

"Dozens of 'em," replied Owen; "but they didn't find much, and it soon petered out. Why, one boy told me he'd hunted two whole days, and found just three mussels, which didn't turn up a single pearl. He said we'd cleaned the whole river out, and sometimes I think that way myself."

"But that bunch back of Ted were as smart as anything, too," observed Max. "Think of them finding that there was a whole lot of ginseng growing wild in the woods around Carson, and gathering it in on the sly."

"They sold it for a snug little sum, too," Owen admitted; "and then started to plague the life out of us. But we came out of the large end of the hole, didn't we, fellows!"

Chatting in this strain they tugged away, and continued to mount higher up toward the headwaters of the sinuous river. But the Big Sunflower was an odd sort of a tributary; in fact, like the Missouri, it should really have been called the main stream, or as Steve expressed it, the "whole push."

"I've been told that it runs right along into the next county, and sometimes spreads itself into a bouncing lake. Why, right where Catamount Island lies, the river is three times as broad as the Evergreen at Carson."

It was Max himself who volunteered this bit of information. They had been keeping at this steady paddling for some hours now, and Bandy-legs was not the only one who grunted from time to time, as he looked at blistered hands, and felt of his sore arm muscles.

"Well, we don't mean to keep on that far, I hope, fellers," remarked Bandy-legs, pathetically, at which Steve laughed in derision.

"You'd sure be a dead duck long before we crossed the border, my boy!" he cried.

"Keep a good lookout ahead," advised Max, some time later.

"He means that the island can't be far away, and by the jumping Jehoshaphat, boy, I think I can see something that looks just like an island around that bend yonder," and Steve pointed with his extended paddle, as he spoke so enthusiastically.

A cheer broke forth, even if it did sound rather weak, for the paddlers were a little short of wind right then. It was the island, sure enough; and as they picked up new vim at the prospect of being soon allowed to rest their weary muscles and backs, the boys examined the place and its surroundings with considerable interest.

They then exchanged looks that meant volumes. Indeed, if Catamount Island did have a bad name, it seemed to deserve all that. The trees were very dense, and made the place look gloomy, and as Bandy-legs declared, "spooky." Several had partly fallen during some heavy blow, and rested upon others that had proven better able to stand up against the wind. A few were fashioned in weird shapes, too; and to tell the truth, it looked as if Nature had taken pains to gather together on that one particular island all the freak things possible.

21

"What do you think of it, boys?" asked Max, smiling a little as he noted how even bold Steve was just a little bit awed by the gruesome aspect of the place which they meant to make their stamping ground for a full week, unless they wished to bring down upon their heads the scorn and derision of Herb and his crowd, and hear their cries of "I told you so; who's a scare-cat now?"

Then Steve gritted his teeth after his usual fashion, and laughed, though truth to tell, there was not any too much mirth about that mockery of a laugh.

"Come on, who cares for expenses! Me to be the first to put a foot on our island," he called out, as he dropped his paddle into the water again, and urged his little buoyant canvas canoe onward with vigorous sweeps.

"*Our* island! Listen to him, would you? Oh! like that, now. As for me, you don't hear me claiming a foot of the old place. Ugh! it's enough to make a fellow shiver just to look at it. And it smells like cats or skunks lived around here. But if the rest of you are bound to go ashore, I suppose I'll have to follow suit. But I'm glad I said good-by to everybody before I came up here."

Nobody paid any attention to what Bandy-legs was saying, as just then they were making for the lower shore of the island, where a fair landing place seemed to offer its services.

The rest were all ashore and looking around, before Bandy-legs managed to jump out of his cranky cedar canoe. He acted as though glad at least to have arrived safe and sound, if very sore.

Pretty soon the whole of them were as busy as beavers, putting up the two tents on ground which Max had selected as suitable for the camp. In doing this he had to consider a number of things, such as a view of the river, nearness to the boats, a chance for drainage in case of a summer storm that might otherwise flood them out, and soak everything they owned; and such matters that an old and experienced camper never fails to remember in the start.

Then came the delightful task of getting the first meal. That is always a pleasure, though it begins to pall upon the party before the weekend. Everybody wanted to have a hand in that first meal, and so Max fixed it that they could enjoy the privilege to their heart's content.

And after the night had closed in around them, what joy to sit around with the dancing and crackling fire, while they brought forward recollections of other occasions when they partook of camp fare, and looked forward to a period of keenest enjoyment.

Even Bandy-legs seemed for the time being to have quite overcome his feeling of timidity and uneasiness, so that he laughed with the rest, and appeared as joyous as anybody, sitting there and watching the curling flames eat deep into the dry wood that had been tossed to them, and feeling so restful after the meal.

Steve was filled with complete happiness. Somehow or other he seemed to be more set than any of his chums upon proving to Herb and his comrades, that they had been a lot of chumps who were almost afraid of their own shadows. He had never been in a gayer mood, Max thought.

Presently all sorts of sounds arose around them, among which were the cries of night birds like the whip-poor-will; owls started to hoot back somewhere on the island; giant frogs boomed forth their calls for "more rum, more rum!" and altogether there was soon quite a noisy chorus under full blast.

But as all these sounds were familiar to even Bandy-legs, though it was not often they heard them in concert, no one remarked that he objected to them.

Max was just in the act of declaring that if there was one dish of which he was particularly fond it was frogs' legs, and that he meant to start on a hunt for some of those blustering fellows in the morning, when a shriek that was entirely different from anything else, broke upon their startled ears.

In spite of all their boasted self command, Steve, Owen, as well as Max, Toby and Bandy-legs scrambled to their feet, and looked at each other speechlessly, while their faces certainly took on a degree of pallor that was remarkable, considering how red were the flames of the fire that tried to paint their cheeks a rosy hue.

CHAPTER IV.

THE SUDDEN AWAKENING.

"Oh! what do you suppose that was?" demanded Bandy-legs, his voice quivering.

"It might have been a wild-cat," suggested Owen, cautiously, as if trying to recall just what he had read about the cries of these animals, when roaming the woods at night.

"Mebbe it was an owl!" remarked Toby, actually forgetting to stammer in his new alarm.

"Max, whatever do you think?" asked Steve, turning on the boy he addressed; for if any one could know it ought to be Max.

"Well, to tell the honest truth, fellows, I'm nearly as much in the dark as the rest of you," admitted Max, looking perplexed.

"But then you've had experience, and ought to know what sort of racket a bobcat makes when he's on the rampage?" insisted Steve, belligerently.

"On the rampage! My goodness!" echoed Bandy-legs, at the same time making sure to move still closer to the blaze; for he suddenly recollected that nearly all the really dangerous beasts of the wilds are afraid of fire.

"It came so suddenly, and lasted so short a time, that I didn't have much of a chance to make up my mind," Max went on; "but if you really want me to say what I suspect made it, I will."

"Go on," Steve said, encouragingly, "I guess we can stand it all right."

He had picked up the shotgun which Max had thought best to bring along, though not expecting to use it in shooting any game like rabbits, squirrels, partridges or quail, since summer was the off season for such things. And when Steve became excited he looked very warlike indeed. Why, Bandy-legs began to feel more confidence just by looking at the ferocious expression Steve assumed. It was good to feel that you had a "fighting chum" nearby, in time of need.

"Yes, let's have it, Max; we're ready to hear the worst," Owen went on.

"It sounded more like a human voice than anything else I can think of!" was what Max immediately said, very calmly indeed.

"Just what I thought you'd give us!" cried Steve, making a move as though ready to spring away into the surrounding darkness, gun in hand.

"Hold on," added Max, taking a firm hold on the coat of the impulsive chum; "we'd like to know why you try to run off, when I remarked that I thought it mightn't be an animal at all, but a human being?"

"Why?" repeated the other, struggling a little as if wanting to break away, but finally giving up the effort, "because I just know who it is, that's what, and I'd give a heap to lay my hands on him, that's all."

"B-b-but, Steve, mebbe the r-r-rest of us'd l-l-like to know, too," stammered Toby, eagerly.

"Yes, and sure you wouldn't be rushing off like a house afire, to leave us here without the gun, while you lost yourself in all this tangled undergrowth," Owen suggested, reproachfully.

Steve looked a little conscience stricken.

"That's right, it would be mean of me, fellows," he admitted, as he glanced at the gun he had snatched up so eagerly. "And likewise silly in the bargain, because in this pitch darkness I'd like as not only stub my toe, and take a beastly header into some snake hole. I guess I'll simmer down, and stay where I'm most needed."

"But, Steve," complained Bandy-legs, "you ain't told us yet who you believe it was made all that noise? And do you think he did it just to give us a scare?"

"Just what I do, Bandy-legs," replied the other, stoutly; "because the feller I had in my mind was Ted Shafter."

"What's that; Ted Shafter!" echoed Bandy-legs, aghast.

"Or if not him, then Shack Beggs, or Amiel Toots!" went on Steve, doggedly nodding his stubborn head up and down, as though the idea had secured a firm footing in his mind, and would not easily be dislodged.

Owen turned to his cousin Max. Somehow, in moments of sudden need, it was noticeable how they all seemed to place great dependence on Max.

"Could that be so, Max?" he asked. "Would you think that bunch of fellows'd take the trouble to come all the way up here just to bother us?"

"Oh! so far as bothering us went, I believe they'd go to even more trouble than that," was the reply Max made. "The only question in my mind is, whether they'd have the nerve to come over to this island at night time, just to try and give us a little turn."

"Of course they knew all about what we expected to do?" suggested Owen.

"We can be sure of that," replied his cousin. "In the first place, Shack Beggs was in that mob that saw us get under way. Then again either Shack, or some other boy in his crowd, must have managed to get into our clubhouse last night after we left, and bored that hole through the bottom of the cedar canoe, thinking we wouldn't notice it."

"Wonder they didn't slash a knife through the canvas boats in the bargain," commented Touch-and-go Steve, gloomily; "it'd be just like their meanness."

"Well, that would have been so barefaced that of course the whole town would have been up in arms, and somebody might tell on them, which'd mean that Ted would be sent away to the reform school for a time," Max explained.

By degrees the boys began to settle down again. Owen was the first to drop back into the comfortable position he had occupied at the time that weird screech first shocked them, and brought about a sudden rising up.

Max managed to possess himself of his gun, and then Steve, quieting down, followed the example of his campmates, by picking out a good place near the crackling blaze, where he could hug his knees, and stare gloomily into the fire.

For some little time the boys exhibited a degree of nervous tension. It was as though they half expected that awful cry to be repeated, or some other event come to pass. But as the minutes glided by without anything unusual happening, by slow degrees their confidence returned, and finally they were chatting at as lively a rate as before the alarm.

All sorts of speculations were indulged in concerning the possible character of the origin of the sound. Bandy-legs in particular was forever springing questions on Max as to what he thought it could have been, if not one of that Shafter crowd.

"Do they have real panthers around here, Max?" he asked suddenly.

"Well, I don't think there's been one seen for a good many years," replied the other, accommodatingly. "Time was, of course, when they need to roam all about this region; yes, and wolves and buffalo as well; but those were in the old days when it was called the frontier."

"Buffalo!" echoed Bandy-legs, in amazement; "why, Max, I always thought buffalo were only found away out West on the plains, where they used to be seen in great big droves, before Buffalo Bill cleaned them out, supplying meat for the workers building the first railroad across the continent."

"Well, that's where you were away off," answered the other, "because in all the accounts in history about Daniel Boone and the early settlers along the Ohio and in Kentucky you can read of them hunting buffalo. Seems they went in pairs or small droves at that time. Why, they used to get them for meat in the mountains of Pennsylvania when on the way across to the valleys on the other side. And at that time there were more panthers around here than you could shake a stick at."

"You'd never ketch me doing that same thing, if it was a panther," admitted Bandy-legs, frankly. "I'm afraid of cats of all kinds the worst ever. Why, I always said I'd rather face six lions than one tiger, any day."

"Sure, who wouldn't?" remarked Steve, dryly. "They'd make way with a feller all the sooner, and end the agony. But Max says he don't believe it could have been a panther, so make your mind easy, Bandy-legs."

They managed to talk of other things in between, but the boy with the short legs would every little while think up some new question in connection with that shriek, which he would fire at Max, and demand an answer. When Steve tried to make fun of him for harping on that old string so long, the other immediately took up arms in his own defense.

"Huh! it's easy enough for you to act like that, Steve," he remarked once, when the other gave him a jeering laugh; "because if we had to make a bolt for it, you've got running legs, and could put out at a whoopin' lick; but how about poor me? Wouldn't I get left behind, and that'd mean make a meal for the big woods cat? Guess I've got more at stake than any of the rest."

But taking it all in all, that first evening spent around the camp fire on Catamount Island was rather enjoyable. Old recollections of other days came cropping up from time to time, and were mentioned, to be commented on. And never before had a blazing fire seemed more delightful than just then. It is always so with those who go out into the wilderness to get close to Nature; the new experience has charms that no other could quite possess.

After a time, however, some of the boys began to yawn at a great rate, as though getting sleepy. None of them had slept any too well on the preceding night, simply because of the excitement they were laboring over, with a week of outing before them.

"Move we get ready to turn in!" suggested Max, finally, when he began to fear lest Bandy-legs in particular would dislocate his jaws, and bring down a new catastrophe on their heads.

"When we drew lots for tents, it turned out that Steve, Bandy-legs and myself were to bunk in this big tent, while Max and Toby, taking a lot of the stuff along, had to sleep in the other, wasn't that it?" remarked Owen, as he got on his feet, and stretched himself, as though a little cramped from sitting so long in one position.

"J-j-just w-w-what it was," Toby replied.

"That makes three of us in our tent, don't it?" said Bandy-legs, as if relieved to know that he would have a companion on either side, for at such times there is safety in numbers.

"Yes, and if that panther does come, he'll have some trouble picking you out in the crowd," jeered Steve.

"That's mean, Steve," declared Max, who saw that Bandy-legs was really concerned, and also remembered that in times gone by the other had spoken more than once of the strange fear he from childhood had entertained for cats of all kinds, while accustomed to playing with every species of dog known to lads.

"Oh! I take it back," quickly responded Steve, who could say sharp things, and then be sorry the minute afterwards.

Of course, having had considerable experience by now, all the boys knew just how to go to work in order to make themselves comfortable, with only a thick camping blanket to serve as a bed.

Max had long ago showed the greenhorns how to fold this, so that while one part lay between their bodies and the ground, they would have several thicknesses over them, to be pulled up as the night grew cooler. Besides, each boy had a rubber poncho in which the blanket could be wrapped during the day, to keep it from getting wet while in the canoes. This was always first of all laid down on the ground, so as to keep the dampness from giving them rheumatism, for even boys may be taken with this ailment, if careless in times when the ground is far from dry.

Everybody else being disposed of, and ready to go to sleep, Max fixed their fire after the manner of a woodsman, so that it would burn for hours, yet never threaten to get away into the woods, should a heavy wind arise.

"All ready, boys?" he asked, feeling his own eyes getting heavy.

A couple of sleepy replies came from the tent where the three chums lay; evidently Toby and Bandy-legs were already far gone in the Land of Nod.

So Max crawled into his snug retreat, and settled himself down to securing some of the refreshing slumber he so much needed.

He had left a flap of the tent up, so that as he lay there he could see out, but as the fire did not come within the range of his vision, he was not annoyed by its flickering. Now and then the flames would spring up, and the vicinity be brightly illuminated; then they would gradually die down again, and things become more indistinct.

Max remained there awake, for some little time; because, as often happens, his sleepiness seemed to desert him after he lay down. Many pleasant things flitted through his mind, for the most part connected with past events in which he had figured, and in quite a number of them having been enjoyed in the company of these four good chums of camp fire and trail.

Then Max went to sleep. He had wondered whether they would be left to pass the night in peace, or be suddenly aroused by some clamor, such as had possibly given Herb and his crowd their scare. Hence, being on the watch for some such alarm, Max was not altogether astonished when he found himself suddenly aroused by a whoop, and heard Bandy-legs shouting out at the top of his voice:

"Help! help! something grabbed me by the leg, and was pulling me out of the tent. I'd have been a goner only I grabbed Steve here, and held on. Get a light, fellers. Where are you all! Hurry up, or it'll come back again after me!"

CHAPTER V.

EXPLORING THE ISLAND.

There was little time wasted in getting outside the two tents; almost before the last of the excited Bandy-legs' complaint had sounded, five shivering boys made their appearance alongside the fire, clad only in their pajamas.

Max had his gun in his hands. He may have carried it out more as a precaution, or to keep the impulsive Steve from dodging in after it, than from any great expectation of finding a use for the weapon. And then again, its appearance would go far toward reassuring poor Bandy-legs that the fear of the unknown beast returning to drag him away was reduced to a minimum.

Steve immediately made a pounce for the fire. Max thought he meant to knock it together, and perhaps induce it to flare up, so as to give them more light; but it seemed that the other was only after a smoldering bit of wood, which he swung around his head until it burst into a flame.

"Now, let it try and attack us, that's all!" cried Steve, as though quite ready to use his novel weapon after the manner of a baseball club, should a vicious bobcat emerge from the dark circle around them, and attempt any "funny business," as Steve called it.

It was thoughtful Owen who stooped down, and threw a little inflammable fuel on the remains of the camp fire, so that when it blazed up, which immediately happened, there was no longer darkness near the spot, as they could see far into the jungle that lay on the side away from the water.

"Now, what happened?" asked Max, turning on Bandy-legs for an explanation.

"Why, here's the way it was, fellers," replied that worthy, bent on squaring himself with his chums; "I was dreamin' of bein' home, when the old tomcat got a sudden notion that I'd been and stepped on his tail. Gee; he turned on me like a flash, and grabbed me by the leg. Seemed like he was changed into a big striped tiger, then and there, for he started to drag me away, like he meant to eat me up. I got hold of the leg of the table, and held on like all get-out. That's when I waked up, and found that I was bein' yanked out of my blanket by some critter that did have hold of my left ankle. And it was Steve and not the table leg I'd been hangin' on to like grim death."

"I should say you had," muttered the one mentioned, who was now rubbing his arm where Bandy-legs had pinched it, "and if you left a piece of skin as big as a fifty-cent piece below my elbow, I'll be glad, believe me. Bet you I'll be black and blue for a week of Sundays. You sure did give me the worst scare I ever had, with that whoop right in my ear, and then grabbin' me like a bear might."

"And l-l-listen to him, w-w-would you," remarked Toby, "he s-s-says he was d-d-dreaming, fellers!"

"After this I vote that we tie Bandy-legs up, head and heels, with the rope we brought along," ventured the aggrieved Steve, pulling up the sleeve of his pajamas to see what the damage might really be. "If he's going to dream about cats going mad, and bust our nice sleep all to flinders in this way, why give him that small tent to himself. Blessed if I want him for a tentmate again."

"But, Steve, I tell you it wasn't a dream after all; only I just happened to get things mixed, you see. Somethin' did grab me by the leg, and try to pull me out of the tent! If I'd been scared so I couldn't kick and yell, why chances are you'd be short one camp-mate right now, that's all."

"Shucks!" grumbled Steve, hard to convince, "talk is cheap; prove it, Bandy-legs!"

"I will, then!"

With that the other dropped down on the ground and started to roll up the left leg of his loose pajamas. He did so with a certain amount of confidence, as though he felt positive that he would be able to display such evidence, that even skeptical Steve might not dispute.

"Now, how about that?" demanded Bandy legs? triumphantly.

All of them lowered their heads to look. And a variety of exclamations attested to the fact that apparently Bandy-legs had carried his point.

"Scratches, as sure as anything!" commented Owen, seriously.

"Fresh done, too, ain't they?" demanded the victim, energetically, determined to clinch matters beyond all chance for dispute, while about it.

"That's right, they are," Max chimed in with.

"P'r'aps if you looked sharp now, one could see where claws had raked me through the leg of my pajamas," suggested Bandy-legs, satisfied to have cleared himself of the charge of having aroused his campmates simply because he happened to be visited with a bad dream.

"Well, I can't just say that's clear," Max continued, "but it looks like something had had hold of you by the ankle, just like you say, Bandy-legs."

"And just add to that, it was pullin' me along in a big hurry, Max. Say, didn't I tell you that if there was anybody goin' to be eat up by cats, it'd be me?" wailed the victim of the night assault.

"That's all right, Bandy-legs," said Steve, in a tone meant to be cheering; "you know we've got a good rope along, and if you only choose to take the trouble to tie yourself to the tent pole every night, nothin' can't run away with you."

Max had to laugh at the idea; and somehow that seemed to rather make things look a bit more cheerful. He made Bandy-legs show him just where he had been lying, and as it was between the other pair, it certainly seemed singular why any intruder should have picked the short-legged boy out for attention.

After Max had gone down on all fours, holding the lantern, which Owen had lighted, and seemed to be trying to discover the trace of feet, he shook his head.

"Perhaps there might have been tracks," he remarked, "but we've moved about so much since, that they've just been covered up."

"Tracks of what, the catamount?" asked Bandy-legs, anxiously.

"Perhaps human tracks!" Max went on.

"There! I expected something like that!" burst out Steve. "If there was anything around here that gripped hold of Bandy-legs, and tried to yank him out of the tent, I'd be willing to wager a heap that it could be laid at the door of them measly critters, Ted Shafter and his gang!"

The others hardly knew what to think. But at any rate the fact that Max had ventured to propose such a solution to the strange mystery of the night assault seemed to give the victim more or less comfort. He could stand being made an object of attack on the part of prank-loving boys, but the very thought of having been seized by a hungry man-eating panther gave him a cold chill.

"Say, do we crawl back in our nice blankets, and try to get some more sleep?" asked Steve, who was shivering; because the air seemed cold, after being so rudely aroused, and made to leave a warm nest.

"Couldn't we just stick it out around the fire?" asked Bandy-legs, who doubtless had conceived a notion that he would feel ever so much safer if awake, and dressed, than lying there helpless, and at the mercy of every beast that chose to creep into the camp.

"I was just going to propose that, boys," remarked Max; "because, you see, it's just about peep of day," and he pointed to the east as he spoke, where, upon looking, the others could see a faint seam of light close down near the horizon, which they knew indicated the coming of the sun.

"Well, I declare, the whole night's gone!" declared the surprised Steve.

"Oh! ain't I glad!" breathed Bandy-legs, crawling into the tent to get some of his ordinary garments, such as he was accustomed to wear when on an outing.

The others followed suit, and it was not long before the camp began to assume a busy appearance, with all of the boys bustling about.

"One night gone, anyhow," remarked Max, as he and Owen started preparation for breakfast, all of them owning up to being hungry for the ham and eggs they had decided to enjoy for the first morning meal in camp.

Then, as daylight had fully come, Max seemed to conceive a sudden notion.

"Get one of the others to help you with this, Owen," he remarked. "I'll be back in half an hour, or less."

Although wondering what he had in mind, Owen, being a boy of few words as a rule, did not attempt to question his cousin. He saw him go down to where the canoes lay up on the beach, and launching one of the smaller canvas ones, paddle off. And as he saw Max move along close to the shore of the island, now beginning to be bathed in the first rays of the rising sun, Owen smiled, as though he had guessed the other's mission.

Later on, just as the call to breakfast was given, Max returned, and drew the little canoe up on the beach where the others lay.

"What luck?" asked his cousin, as Max sat down and started to pour himself a tin cup of coffee, his platter having been already filled with fried ham and eggs that sent up a most tempting odor.

The others lifted their heads to listen, and even stopped eating, hungry as they were, to learn what it was Max had been investigating.

"Nothing doing," replied the returned paddler, with a smile. "I went completely around the island, and examined the shore the best way I could, for signs of some boat, or to see where one had landed last night, but I didn't get a glimpse of anything. If they did come off the mainland, they knew how to get ashore without leaving any signs behind, that's all."

"But, Max, I didn't know that Ted Shafter was such a good woodsman as all that!" objected Owen.

"No more he isn't," replied the other, as he lowered his cup, after taking one good drink of the hot contents, that tasted better than anything he ever got at home, where they had thick cream, and delicate china to drink from. "And that's one reason why I'm puzzled to believe it could have been them."

Bandy-legs looked worried again.

Once more his hopes were shattered because, if it turned out the intruder had been an animal after all, what about those six other nights he would have to pass in that tent, with the unfeeling Steve and the heavy-sleeping Owen?

"Well, what are we going to do about it?" demanded the last-named boy.

"I'll tell you," replied Max, in a matter-of-fact tone; "we've got the whole day ahead of us, to prowl around, and see what the blessed old island looks like. And perhaps we might find out a few things before dark comes on again. As I said a while ago, one night's gone. I hope now none of you want to throw up the sponge, and go back home, to let Herb and his crowd crow over us?"

"Not me!" shouted Steve, like a flash.

"And I'm willing to stick it out!" added Owen, firmly.

"M-m-me t-t-too!" put in Toby, who was munching some cold biscuits they had fetched along, and of which he was especially fond.

All of them looked at Bandy-legs, and he could not deny the appeal he saw in the faces of his chums. It made considerable difference, too, now that the bright daylight surrounded them; for even a timid boy can feel brave between sunrise and sunset.

"I'm willing to hold on, if the rest do," he declared, "though it's pretty tough if I'm goin' to be the only one that's in danger of bein' chawed up by savage tomcats that roam about here. But, Max, if we go nosing around to-day, I want to keep close to you, and that bully little gun of yours, understand. Them's my conditions for agreein' to stand pat, and stay here on this haunted island."

"Rats!" scoffed the unbelieving Steve; "haunted, your eye! You mark my words, it'll all turn out just as common as anything, when we once get the hang of things. Ain't it always that way, Max? Didn't it look easy to the old fellers over at the court of Ferdinand and Isabella, when Columbus, he stood an egg on end by just breaking it a little?"

"That's what it did, Steve; and I'm glad to see how you take it," replied Max.

But when a little later they did start out to look around a little, being more than curious, Bandy-legs was allowed to do as he suggested, and keep close company with Max and the twelve-bore gun. He carried in his hand a ferocious-looking fish spear, which he had mounted on a pole about ten feet long. Owen had the hatchet; Toby the long-bladed knife which they used to cut bread and ham with; while Steve patted his pocket in a significant way, as though he carried something there, up to now he had overlooked, but which seemed to give considerable confidence.

In this manner, then, the five boys sallied out to investigate their surroundings, and see what the island with the bad name contained. If they happened to run against some wild-cat, or other savage animal, they wanted to be in shape to put up a good stiff fight.

Max had to laugh when he saw his chums lined up, armed in this fashion.

"I just pity the poor thing that tries to give this crowd trouble," he remarked; "to look at the lot of weapons we carry, you'd think we expected to have a battle for the possession of Catamount Island instead of starting out on a peaceful little exploring expedition."

"All the same, the handling of such things makes a fellow feel better," declared Bandy-legs.

"It may you," burst out Steve, who had been dodging that fish spear right and left for some time, "but if you keep on trying to poke that blooming four-pronged stabber into my eyes, like you've been doing, it won't be much fun for the rest of us. Show him how to carry the thing, Max, if he must take it along."

This being amicably arranged, with Bandy-legs holding the spear part in front of him, so that he might make use of it in an emergency as a lance, they started out. Somehow, no one seemed to consider the possibility of their camp being invaded during their absence. The eatables had been hung up, so that hungry wild-cats might not run away with them should they take a notion to visit the place while the five boys were away; but no one thought of one of their own species coming around.

It was indeed hard work making their way through the dense growth that covered the main part of Catamount Island. Max saw that as the place had been let alone by mankind, Nature had kept on increasing the wild tangle of vines, bushes and saplings that filled the spaces between the larger trees. In some places the branches were so very dense overhead that it seemed gloomy and even "spooky," as Bandy-legs took pains to inform his companions.

Birds they saw many times, and often the whirr of wings announced the sudden flight of a partridge. Squirrels abounded, and even a raccoon was sighted, while Max declared that he felt sure he had a glimpse of the red brush of a vanishing fox that had been disturbed in his day nap by their approach.

Still, all these were such things as they had expected to meet with. What pleased Max most of all was the fact that outside of a few harmless small snakes the island seemed to hardly deserve the terribly bad name it had gained as a breeding spot for venomous reptiles, and which reputation it was that had always kept local hunters from visiting its shores in the season.

The little party was pushing through the thickest part of the jungle, where they had great difficulty in making progress at all, and often tripped over roots, or found themselves twisted up in vines that hung down from the trees, when Max, who led the van, turned and made a motion with his hand that the others new signified he had discovered something to which he wished to call their attention.

And so, filled with eager curiosity, they craned their necks forward in the endeavor to learn just what it was that had apparently aroused the interest of Max so abruptly.

CHAPTER VI.

WHAT THE ASHES TOLD MAX.

"Get back, Steve, and let me have room with my fish spear!" whispered Bandy-legs, nervously, just as if he fully expected that they were about to be attacked by a legion of fierce wild-cats, and wished to be able to impale the first that showed up on his lance.

Steve, fearing for his legs or back, seized hold of the long pole upon which the four-pronged and barbed spear was mounted, then he felt safe in leaning forward again, to see what it was Max had discovered.

"Why, it's a cabin!" he exclaimed, as though somewhat disappointed.

"A cabin!" echoed Bandy-legs; but there was relief rather than chagrin in his voice, and the pole Steve clutched steadied a little.

"Sure it is, and nothing more!" remarked Owen.

"B-b-but, f-f-fellows, did yon ever s-s-see *such* a c-c-cabin?" demanded Toby.

"Well, it does look kind of queer," admitted Steve, "but mebbe that's just because of the shack being abandoned so long. The weeds and grass and bushes have grown right up to the walls; and looky there, the roof even seems to be green, like grass had took root there. She is a dandy-lookin' roost, sure as you're born, Toby."

All of them stared at the odd little affair. Cabins they had seen before now, by scores, some fairly commodious, others small and limited in accommodations, bat never one that looked like this shack on Catamount Island.

"Anybody around, that you can see, Max?" asked Owen, presently, when they had been standing there in that group, watching the green-roofed cabin, and the vegetation-covered walls of the low, squat cabin, for some time.

"Well, if there is, I haven't had a squint of 'em," Steve took occasion to remark, before the one addressed could reply.

"S-s-somebody g-g-give 'em a hail!" said Toby, sensibly.

So Max immediately called out:

"Hello there!"

No response followed. Although the five boys watched eagerly to see if any figure that might correspond with the queer cabin came out of the partly opened door, nothing happened.

"Cabin, ahoy!" sang out Steve, in a very loud, gruff voice, that surely merited some attention, if so be there chanced to be any one at home.

He met with no better success than had attended the salute of Max. The boys exchanged glances, and nodded, as if their minds were made up.

"If the mountain won't come to Mahomet, then he's just got to go to the mountain, that's all," Owen remarked, as he started to push forward.

Every one began to move at the same time, and in this sort of hollow square, with the menacing fish spear gripped by Bandy-legs sticking out ahead, they advanced toward the mysterious cabin.

All was silent around, save that a busy woodpecker hammered loudly on the dead top of a chestnut tree close by, looking for a breakfast of grubs. In this fashion, then, they reached the front of the shack that seemed to have been deserted so long that vegetation was trying to claim, or cover it out of sight.

Max thrust his head in at the partly open door, while the others stood by, ready to back him up, if any ferocious thing attacked him. But apparently he saw nothing of the sort beyond, for after that one survey, Max proceeded to deliberately enter the strange cabin.

The others pushed close on his heels, for they had determined to stick together through thick and thin. Even Bandy-legs, spear and all, tried to gain entrance, but in the end he had to let his pole drop to the ground, since there was hardly room for that inside, and the four boys as well.

They looked around them. The interior of the shack was certainly about as desolate as anything they had ever set eyes on. Not a sign of anything in the way of former comforts seemed to remain. Over in one corner there had at one time been a sort of berth made, where the party who built the cabin kept his blanket most likely and slept; but just now it only had some dead leaves in it, such as might go to serve a wild beast for its nest.

Something flitted out of the opening that served as a window, and from the fleeting glimpse the boys had of this, they believed it must have been a red squirrel, that possibly thought to hide its store of nuts in this lonesome cabin, though as yet the season for this sort of thing was far distant, since summer had not progressed very far.

After all it was Toby, who, as a rule, had little to say, who broke the silence that hung over the chums as they stared around.

"Gee!"

Whether it was that the sound of a human voice had stirred them up, or the fact of Toby saying that one expressive word without stumbling, as usual, something aroused the others, and Steve broke loose.

"Well, of all the tough-looking places I've ever struck, I think this takes the cake!" he exclaimed.

No one ventured to disagree with him on that score, because he expressed just what was in the mind of every one of the others.

"Now whoever could have lived here, do you think?" demanded Bandy-legs, who, now that his alarm was of the past, could appear as curious as the next one.

Max was using his eyes to look about. He was always quick to discover things that would escape the observation of his companions. It had become a settled habit with Max to always be on the alert in cases like this, so as to pick up valuable information, even from small things. The secrets of the trail he dearly loved to examine, so as to read a story there that was hidden from common eyes.

And so the first thing he discovered was the fact that some animal, or human being, had been eating here not many days back, at least. There were a number of small bones lying scattered about, which in time would naturally be carried away by a prowling fox or wild-cat, or perhaps a raccoon.

He picked a couple of these up, while the other boys watched his actions with interest, expecting that Max would read the signs rightly, and being content to leave that task to his ingenuity.

"A partridge, I should say, though I may be wrong," he remarked, after looking closely at the bone, apparently from the wing of a fairly large bird.

Then he smelled of it, as though that might give him a clew.

"It was cooked before being eaten," he went on, "and that tells the story, fellows. No wild-cat ever ate that partridge, because so far as known they never bother with cooking their food."

"Course not," added Bandy-legs, seriously, not understanding the humor of the remark Max had made; "how d'ye suppose they'd ever be able to build a fire? Tell me that, now, Max. It was hard enough for me to learn how to do it, and I'm human."

"Oh! are you?" snapped Steve, always ready to give the other a sly dig when he saw the chance; "well, now, we're glad to know that, because sometimes we've wondered if it was so, haven't we, fellows?"

Max did not pay any attention to these side remarks. He was still looking about him, as though under the belief that if he hunted closer he might discover other things that would help explain about the strange cabin and its equally mysterious late occupant.

"I think you're right about the partridge part of it, Max," said Owen just then.

"What makes you say that?" asked the other.

"Why, because, while we were on the way here, you remember, I stepped out of the path we were following. That was so I could examine something that had attracted my attention close by, down in the matted bushes."

"What was that something, Owen?" asked the other.

"I've never seen one made of twisted vines before, always cords; but I believe it must have been a partridge snare," replied Owen, confidently.

"That might be," Max went on, in a reflective way. "Suppose, now, some man was on this island, and either couldn't get away, or else for some reason didn't want to go over to the mainland. He'd have to live, some way or other, and if he didn't have a gun and ammunition, why, the only way he could keep alive would be by getting fish from the river, mussels perhaps, for I've seen quite a few shells on the shore, though they looked like they'd been opened by muskrats, or by snaring some of the game birds out of season."

"That sounds pretty good to me, Max," admitted Steve, always ready to express an opinion, one way or the other.

"T-t-to m-m-me same way!" Toby followed.

"A man!" echoed Bandy-legs; and then as a sudden idea struck him, he went on: "Say, Max, looky here, you don't mean that it was a human being grabbed me by the leg last night, and tried to haul me out from under my blanket?"

"I hope not," replied the other; "for any man who would leave the marks of his nails on your ankle like we saw, must be a pretty savage sort, to my way of thinking."

"Wonder when he could have been here last?" remarked Owen, also beginning to look around, as though hoping to discover an answer to his own question.

Bandy-legs was appearing rather uneasy. He could not forget what a tremendous pull he had received at the time he was awakened; and the very thought that they might even now be in the abiding place of the creature that had been responsible for his fright gave him new cause for shivering.

He looked up and around, as though suspecting that the aforesaid human being might be hiding close by, and watching them with ferocious eyes. But there was no loft to the squatty cabin, and hence no place where anybody of size might lie in concealment. Still, Bandy-legs looked longingly down at his fish spear, and wished he had thought to shorten that pole, so he could always keep it handy in case of a sudden necessity.

Max even tried to find traces of footprints on the floor; but as the earth was as hard as rock he did not meet with any flattering success there.

"Anyhow, he had a fire in here, looks like, when he cooked that bird," Steve remarked, as he pointed to a little heap of ashes over where the chimney, that was made of hard mud and pieces of stone, stood.

Max saw that there seemed to be considerable of truth in this discovery of the quick-witted chum. There were certainly ashes there, a little heap of them, and these could not have been left behind when the former occupant of the cabin deserted his home years ago; for the winds of winter, sifting in through the partly open door, would have scattered the ashes long since.

They spoke of more recent occupancy, perhaps within the last month, or even week.

"I reckon, now, this is the cabin that boy spoke about, when they called out after us as we were leaving town?" Max said, half to himself, as he continued to look around him.

"And from the way he talked, you'd sure believe he thought it was the worst kind of a shack he'd ever struck," Owen went on to remark.

"I've been thinking that over," observed Steve, "and come to this conclusion—that they must have started to spend the night in this same cabin, and perhaps the ashes there are some from their fire. Then during the night they got their bad scare, which none of them would ever tell about, on any account. It must have come from *something* that they saw in this same cabin; and whatever it was, it sent the whole bunch on the run for their boat. They said they nearly killed themselves as they bumped into trees, fell over vines, straddled stumps; and when they came back to town they sure looked as if they had been through a fight."

"And this is that queer old cabin he said we'd run across?" ventured Bandy-legs, again turning to cast his eyes about him, this time in more of an awed manner than before, though the shack had not changed its appearance one iota meanwhile.

"But you see, boys," Max remarked, with a smile, "they started to bunk in here, and we don't mean to bother ourselves trying that, when we've got our good tents along. So, after all, I don't see why we shouldn't be able to stick it out the full week, and go back to laugh at Herb."

As he was speaking Max stepped across the interior of the deserted green-roofed cabin. Knowing that some notion had appealed to him, the others watched to see what he would do. They saw him stoop down beside the little pile of gray-looking ashes that lay in the fireplace.

"Watch him!" said Owen, beginning to suspect the truth.

Max thrust his hand down upon the heap; then he quickly moved it so as to further penetrate the ashes; after which he sprang hastily to his feet, exclaiming:

"Of course I don't pretend to say who the party was that devoured that partridge, fellows, but he must have had it for his supper *last night*; and there's been fire here up to this morning, *because the ashes are still warm!*"

CHAPTER VII.

THE MYSTERY OF THE CABIN.

Max, in whose ability to understand all such things they felt so much confidence, spoke those surprising words, the others showed more or less astonishment.

One by one they had to bend down, and put his assertion to the test, by poking a finger gingerly into the little pile of gray ashes. Even Bandy-legs would not rest satisfied until he had thus copied the example of the others.

"Warm-say, it's *hot*, fellers!" he exclaimed, as he hastily snatched back his hand, and commenced to blow the ends of his fingers. "Anyhow, I guess I must 'a' just rooted out a live coal, for it burned like the dickens."

"Well, we know one thing that we didn't before," asserted Owen.

"Two, you'd better say, for they both sting like fun," grumbled Bandy-legs, rubbing his injured fingers vigorously.

"Yes," said Steve, "somebody's been in this old cabin, and not so very long ago, either; for they must have made a little fire about dawn, to fry a part of a partridge by. And if that's been all the poor critter had for his breakfast, I'd like to wager, now, he must be hungry yet."

"I'm glad of one thing," ventured Bandy-legs.

"That you didn't get three fingers scorched; is that it?" asked Steve.

"Naw!" answered the other, indignantly, "Tell you what it is, boys; I didn't believe much of it when they said it was ghosts up here on Catamount Island. Now we know there ain't none around."

"Well, how do you know it, Bandy-legs?" asked Max.

"Because ghosts—whoever heard of them wanting a fire, either to cook with, or else keep warm? Still, that awful howl we heard last night—I keep wonderin' what it meant, fellers?"

No one attempted to answer Bandy-legs. They believed they had about exhausted that subject while sitting around the camp fire on the previous evening, before starting to go to their blankets; and did not feel like reopening the question.

"Let's get out of this," suggested Steve, with a shiver.

"Second the motion," declared Toby, speaking straight again.

"Unless Max wants to hang around a little longer, in the hope of striking a clew that might tell us something about this queer old place, and the mysterious party that's been sleeping here," Owen followed with.

"Oh, I think I'm done looking around in here," the one mentioned remarked, with a shade of disappointment in his voice; for Max disliked to give up any object he had set out to attain.

"We might run across some tracks outside," suggested Steve.

"I meant to give that a try," Max explained; "but somehow I don't feel as if we'd have any great success there; because, when we came in I noticed that the ground was kind of poor for showing footprints—rocky, and covered with dead leaves that have drifted in here right along."

But all the same Max spent some little time hovering around, now down on his knees and closely examining the ground; again looking up at the swaying limbs of the overhanging trees, as though knowing that they could explain the mystery, if only they might speak.

"Any use, Max?" called out impatient Steve, presently; for he had been fretting at the delay for several minutes now.

"Give it up," returned the other, turning his back on the strange cabin with its green roof and lichen-covered walls.

"Which way now?" asked Steve, evidently pleased that they were going to make a move of any sort; for inaction galled him always.

"Back to camp?" queried Bandy-legs, hopefully; because he believed that was the one comfortable spot on all that island, and regretted ever having left it; though they could never have tempted him to remain in camp alone; not on that island with the evil name, at any rate.

"Well, after starting out, we ought to poke around a little farther than we've done this far, I should think," Max replied; "still, I'm ready to do whatever the majority say; three against two has always been our rule. How about it, boys?"

"G-g-go on!" exclaimed Toby, promptly.

"Same here," from Steve.

"Count me in," came from Owen, smilingly; for whatever Max thought right, his cousin could usually be depended on to back up.

"And I move we make it unanimous; because I don't just like being the only one on the other side," Bandy-legs ended up with.

"That settles it, then; so come along, and we'll keep on to the upper end of the island," Max suggested, leading off, gun in hand.

"Oh, wait, I've forgotten something!" cried Bandy-legs, running back.

Steve groaned aloud.

"I just knew he'd remember that blooming old fish spear again!" he declared. "I saw he'd forgotten it, but I didn't say a word; because he keeps turning the thing around so that a fellow don't dare call his life his own. See here, Bandy-legs, let me knock off a few feet from that long pole. Then mebbe you c'n handle the spear better."

"Oh, that's awful kind of you, Steve; I was just thinking of trying to do that myself, when you saved me the trouble," remarked Bandy-legs, sweetly, as he suffered Steve to take the long pole out of his hands, place it on two stones, and by jumping smartly on it at the weakest part, manage to sever some four feet of the spear shaft.

"Now you can handle it better; and for goodness' sake keep it away from my back," Steve went on to say; "there's no telling what you might do, if you got excited all of a sudden; and I wouldn't like to be taken for a big carp, or a sucker either."

So they turned their backs on the queer cabin, and once more plunged into the tangle of vines and vegetation, making their way slowly onward. At times they could not even see the sun that they knew: was shining above the leafy canopy over their heads. But Max seemed to have no difficulty whatever in keeping along a straight course.

"Don't see how he does it," muttered Bandy-legs, as he fumbled with a little compass he carried all the time nowadays; for having been lost once upon a time in the woods, he was determined not to take chances that way again.

"Oh, there are plenty of ways for keeping a course you set, even when the sun is behind the clouds," Max told him. "It's a poor hand that depends alone on seeing sun or moon to know his way in the forest. I can tell from the bark on these trees which is north; then the green moss on the trunks tells me the same thing; and even the general way the trees lean points it out; for you'll notice that nine out of ten, if they bend at all, do so toward the southeast; that's because all of our heavy winter storms come from the northwest."

"All that's mighty interesting, Max," remarked Steve; "wish I knew as much as you do about traveling through the woods, and the things a fellow is apt to meet up with there. The more I hear you tell, the more I make up my mind I'm going to take lessons in woodcraft; but I never seem to fully catch on."

"Well, it comes easier with some persons than with others," remarked Max, who was too kind to say what he really thought; which was that in his opinion boys, or men either for that matter, who are hasty and impetuous by nature, never make clever hands in the woods, where patient labor at times is the only method of solving some of the puzzling things that confront one.

"Now we're getting near the upper end of the island," remarked Owen, a while later.

"How do you find that out!" asked Bandy-legs, looking around him helplessly, as if he really expected to see signposts to the right and left, informing the traveler of the lay of the land.

"Why," answered Owen, "you see, the trees are getting lower, and not so thick, as the soil doesn't seem so rich down near the water. I can see through the upper branches here, and we couldn't do that before. Besides, I've been keeping tabs on the distance we came, measured by paces; and I reckon we just must be near the other end of the island by now. Max said it was about two hundred and fifty yards from top to bottom."

"Oh, is that it?" was all Bandy-legs remarked; but he beamed admiringly on Owen from that moment, as though he might be sharing the halo of glory that was hovering over the head of Max.

They did come out on the shore a couple of minutes later. Looking up the river it was easy to see where the stream became narrow again, after spreading out into the broad bay where Catamount Island was situated.

"And to think we've just got to go back that same way," sighed Bandy-legs, dismally.

"Perhaps not," remarked Max, who had a frown on his face, as of new concern. "I was just thinking that we'd better keep right along the beach here, boys, and get back to camp as soon as we can. I reckon we've been gone more than a full hour now; and that we may have done a foolish thing to come away, and leave things unprotected."

"Whew, that *was* silly of us, sure enough!" ejaculated Steve; "and yet it never struck me that way till you mentioned it, Max. Yes, let's lose no more time, but get a move on us. Looks like we might have easy walking all the way, and get there in next to a jiffy."

"If so be those Shatters and Toots and Beggs are around, haven't we left things nice for them, though?" commented Owen. "If we're lucky enough to get off scot free this time, you won't catch us doing just that sort of foolish thing again."

"They might steal our grub!" gasped Bandy-legs, to whom such a thing would be in the nature of a terrible calamity, since he did like good eating above almost anything else.

"What about our canoes?" said Max, sternly, very much provoked at himself for having made this slip, when the others all seemed to look to him to provide against any such mistake in judgment.

They hurried as much as the rough nature of the shore line allowed. Poor Bandy-legs was put to it to keep up with his more nimble companions; and came puffing along in the rear, sometimes tripping over the pole of his fish spear, but holding on to the same with dogged determination.

And so, in the course of a little time, they rounded the point that stood out just above where they had fixed their camp, and thus came in sight of the beach upon which they had landed when reaching Catamount Island the afternoon before.

CHAPTER VIII.

AN UNWELCOME DISCOVERY.

"Bully, they're still there, just like we left them!" shouted Steve; and from the manner in which he said this, it was evident that he had shared in some of the fears which beset his companions.

In fact, all of the boys experienced a singular relief when they discovered that the canoes still lay there on the beach.

"Seems to be all hunky dory," Bandy-legs was heard to remark, as he came puffing along in the rear, determined to keep up with the procession; "if only now them tricky fellers ain't gone and bored more auger holes in my little cedar dinky! You never can tell. 'Pearances are often deceitful, remember, we used to write in our copybooks at school? Well, they are, sometimes. I know it, because I never 'spected to have the river come in on me; and it did, you just bet it did!"

But while Bandy-legs was amusing himself by this manner of talk, no one was apparently paying the least attention to him. They had hurried along, eager to get to the camp, and verify their first impression, to the effect that all was well.

So far as they could see, as they drew near, things were just as they had left them something like an hour and a half previously. The two tents stood there, with the little burgees flapping idly in the morning breeze. Possibly a wandering 'coon or a curious fox may have dropped in to investigate conditions; but the food had all been placed far above the reach of such hungry creatures, so no one need feel the least bit of alarm.

It was Max who made the first discovery that set them to quivering again with a new apprehension.

"Look at the flap of the tent here!" he exclaimed. "I'm dead sure I fastened it tight behind me; and I was the last one in there. It's hanging loose, right now!"

"Wow, so's ours!" whooped Steve, furiously.

The boys plunged into the tents, anxious once more concerning the state of affairs; and immediately a chorus of indignant outcries told that they found things otherwise than satisfactory.

"Somebody's been rooting around in here!" called out Steve, from the depths of the second tent.

"And mauled all our duds, too! Look at the stuff scattered around, would you?" Bandy-legs was heard to howl.

"Looks like the thief wanted to find something or other, and must have been frightened off by hearing us coming," Owen declared, also a bit angrily.

As yet there had come no loud outcries from the other tent; but that was not because those who had rushed inside found things just to their satisfaction. Max was always a fellow of few words; and as for Toby, he never could express himself intelligently when tremendously excited. He just stood there, with his lower jaw moving up and down, yet no sound following the action.

There was good reason for this feeling of dismay on the part of the pair occupying the smaller tent, where most of the provisions were kept. For they had discovered, as soon as they entered, that everything was thrown about, helter-skelter. Indeed, it looked as though the unknown thief must have been gathering together pretty much all their supplies in the shape of foodstuff, with the evident intention of carrying the same off; when, alarmed by their coming, he had grabbed up a strip of breakfast bacon, the last loaf of bread, and possibly a can of baked beans, with which he had hastily decamped.

Max, after the first flush of his indignation had passed away, was rather amused than otherwise by the affair. The loss had not been so very great after all, since no damage had been done to the precious canoes. And if it came to the worst, one of the campers could easily be dispatched to the home town to buy more provisions, since they had plenty of money still in the treasury, thanks to those wonderful little pearls, taken from the waters of this same Big Sunflower River.

As usual with him, Max began to cast around in order to find some clew to the identity of the thief. Of course the other three had by this time hurried into the smaller tent to ascertain what the extent of the damages might be. And loud were the wailings of Bandy-legs when he heard that among the missing things was the splendid strip of bacon, on which he had cast many an envious eye, as he contemplated future enjoyment, with slices of the same sizzling in a hot frying pan, and sending off the odors that made him positively ravenous with hunger.

"Oh, but wasn't it good we came back just in time!" he exclaimed, as he looked around at the untidy interior of the tent, with a pile of provisions lying in the open center, where the eager intruder had thrown them. "He meant to just clean us out, that's what he did. I bet that Herb Benson had something to do with this mean old raid. He wanted to scare us off the island, or starve us out!"

If Max thought along these same lines he had not as yet mentioned the fact; but he did look queerly at Bandy-legs when he said this last sentence, as though the possibility of such a thing appealed to him.

"Was there only one feller here, or a crowd?" demanded Steve, as he eyed the pile of canned goods, that ham that was only partly cut, and a number of packages containing prunes, sugar, flour and such things, many of them as yet not even opened.

"Looks like there was half a dozen; or else the feller, if there was only one, had an appetite that would beat Bandy-legs here all holler," declared Steve, who was really more enraged than any of the others.

All of them looked to Max to decide this question, satisfied that if the truth could be learned at all, he would unearth it.

"I think there was only a single thief here," he presently said. "And I'll tell you why I hit on that. He certainly carried off a few things, just as much as he could grab up in a big hurry when he heard us. Now, his first intention was to scoop in the whole business; you can see how he piled the stuff up here, meaning to get it all. And if there had been two, three, or more, they'd have made a bigger hole in our grub department than happened."

"That sounds good to me, Max," remarked Owen, nodding his head attentively.

Toby was here heard to make a jumble of sounds, being still too excited to get his vocal cords in decent working order. He kept pointing at a nail that had been driven into the tent pole.

Now, strange to say, Steve was really the quickest to understand what the stammering boy meant, when he became twisted up in this way.

"He says his sweater is gone, the dark-blue one that his guardian, Mr. Jackson, gave him just a week ago on his birthday. And he left it hanging there on that old nail," was Steve's explanation of the strange jumble of sounds Toby was giving forth.

"And that's true every word of it," put in Max at that moment; "for just as I turned to quit this tent, as we were going off, that same sweater fell down off the nail. I stopped long enough to hang it up again. So if it's gone, the thief took a notion he could make good use of it."

Toby remained silent with indignation for a long time; and in his case this was not a mere figure of speech either, but a grim reality, for he was tongue-tied.

"Let Max hunt around, and see if there are any tracks," said Owen.

"That's the ticket!" added Bandy-legs; and both the others nodded their heads in immediate approval of the scheme.

Whenever it came down to a showing of woods lore, Max was the one always designated to handle the matter. His chums believed him capable of discovering almost anything going, if only a few faint tracks had been left behind.

Nothing loth, Max started in to look; but he knew in the beginning that the task would be a difficult one, and the results not at all equal to the exertion put forth.

Still he did find several places where a footprint, not at all like any made by their own shoes, seemed to tell where the intruder had stepped, in making his rapid rounds of the camp.

"There was only one thief, boys," he announced, after he had looked carefully.

"Man or boy, do you think, Max?" asked Owen.

"A man; and I should say a pretty hefty one, too," replied the other, with conviction in his voice.

"Why, how c'n you tell that, Max, without ever once gettin' sight of the feller?" demanded the astonished Bandy-legs.

"Oh, shucks, how dense some people are!" put in Steve, scornfully. "Why, stands to reason, don't it, that a big man'd wear shoes ever so much longer than a little man, or a kid? Well, look at that print Max is pointing to right now! Don't think any Shafter, Toots or Beggs made that, do you?"

"Gosh!" exclaimed Bandy-legs, staring; "he must 'a' been a giant, sure. I never did see a bigger shoe print, honest now. And, boys, it ain't the nicest thing going to know that monster is right here, marooned on this island with us."

"Now what makes you say that, Bandy-legs?" demanded Steve. "How d'ye know but what he come across from the mainland?"

"Why," the other hastened to say, as though proud of having his opinion asked, "he'd have to swim, then, because Max here said there wasn't a sign of a boat landin' anywhere along the shore. Fact is, the island is so rough that boats would find it pretty hard to land anywhere, but on this little beach right at the foot, and made just for such a thing. And then again, Steve, don't you forget about that queer old cabin, now. He lives there, sure as you're born!"

"Whew, six more nights!"

That was Toby Jucklin finally getting his breath; and as there was no telling when he would talk steadily, or stammer, none of his campmates thought it at all strange to hear him say these words calmly and evenly. Toby had been wrestling with those miserable vocal cords of his for so long a time that he now had them under control for a short period at least.

"Can we stand it, fellows?" asked Owen, more to find out how the others felt than because his faith was becoming wobbly.

"Sixty, if you said the word!" declared the impulsive Steve, grimly; "why, after accepting that dare, a dozen critters like this one we haven't ever seen yet couldn't frighten *me* away from Catamount Island; no siree, bob!"

Max looked admiringly, also affectionately at the speaker. If there was one trait he liked about Steve, it was his indomitable pluck. The boy was absolutely afraid of nothing that walked, flew, or crawled. He was as bold as a lion, but very indiscreet. He often reminded Max of a small terrier attacking a big St. Bernard, and snapping viciously all the while. Yes, Steve was a bundle of nerves, and not to be daunted.

"I honestly believe you would stick it out if it took all summer, Steve," he remarked, laying a hand on the other's arm.

"Excuse me, then," declared Bandy-legs. "This thing wears on my nerves like everything. I'll soon be skin and bones if it keeps up. Somebody tell me what that big thief wanted with me last night, when he grabbed my leg, and started to haul me out of the tent? That's what bothers me. He seems to've got a spite against me in particular. I bet you he's got his wicked eye on me, right at this blessed minute."

"Oh, p'r'aps he thought it was a ham he grabbed hold of," remarked Steve, flippantly, as he pointed to Bandy-legs' rather plump lower limbs, of which he was rather vain, in spite of their shortness.

But for once Bandy-legs did not laugh at a joke that was on himself. The matter appeared too serious for trifling. How could he ever go to sleep peacefully when expecting to be aroused suddenly by a terrible tug, and feel himself being dragged along the ground, just as though seized by a striped tiger of the East Indian jungle?

"I see there's only one way to be on the safe side," he was muttering disconsolately; "I've just got to come to tying myself to the tent pole every night Then if he drags me off, down comes the old tent; and I guess the rest of you'll sit up and take notice at that."

"You might shin out for home, Bandy-legs?" suggested Steve, just to test the sticking quality of the other.

"But I won't, all the same," flashed Bandy-legs, with a determined shake of his head. "If the rest of yer c'n stand havin' that sort of business goin' on, reckon I ought to hold out. But I wish now I'd brought a gun along. Then mebbe he'd let me alone, or take a feller of his size."

"Come along, boys, let's get things in shipshape again, and see just what's gone!" called out Max, who believed in looking things squarely in the face, and then making the best out of a bad bargain.

So the campers started with a vim to put things as they were before the visit of the unknown forager, who seemed destined to occupy Catamount Island with them during the balance of their stay.

CHAPTER IX.

WATCHED FROM THE SHORE.

The day passed slowly.

Somehow no one seemed very anxious to stray very far away from the camp. For one thing it was out of the hunting season; and on this account the presence of many partridges on the island could not lure Max. They had stirred up quite a number while making that little hike toward the upper end of the place; and every time a bird was flushed, going off with a sudden roar of wings, Bandy-legs had weakened; so that by the time they got back home again he felt as though he had been through a spell of sickness.

And then to have that new sensation sprung upon them, and find that an unknown prowler had paid them a visit in their absence, was, as Bandy-legs expressed it, "too, too much."

But because the boys lounged around camp was no reason why they were not enjoying themselves hugely. Why, even Bandy-legs tried to forget all the dreadful nights ahead of them still, six in a row, and find some source of amusement.

Each fellow seemed, as the afternoon glided along, to just naturally gravitate toward the kind of pleasure that interested him most.

Max and Owen were examining some small animal tracks every little while, which the latter would find along the edge of the water; and as his knowledge of such things lay in the form of book learning, while his cousin had had considerable experience in a practical way, he invariably, after puzzling his head awhile, softly called to Max, who willingly joined him.

Now it was a muskrat that had wandered along the edge of the river, looking no doubt for a fresh shellfish for his supper. Then again, Max proved beyond a shadow of a doubt that a raccoon had crept up to the edge of the water at a place where an old log thrust out. Here he could lie flat, and fish with his paw for a stray small bass that happened to pass too close to the shore for its safety.

The third set of tracks, differing materially from both of the others, Max pronounced the trail of a sly mink; which, with the fisher, is perhaps the boldest and most destructive enemy of the brook trout known.

While these two were amusing themselves in this way, and Owen making notes in his little book all the while, Steve was using the rod and line to some advantage. Perched on the end of another convenient trunk of a fallen tree that projected out over the end of the bank, he managed to secure quite a delightful mess of bass from the passing river—"taking toll," Steve called it.

Toby Jucklin seemed to find his greatest pleasure in taking cat naps. He complained of losing a heap of sleep on the preceding night; and as there was no telling what the second might bring forth, he believed in taking time by the forelock, as he called it.

And Bandy-legs, well, he was sitting there for a long time, working industriously with a pad of paper and a lead pencil; and seemed to be so wrapped up in whatever he was doing that he did not notice Max silently approach, bend down, and secure one of the sheets of paper he had already filled with his crabbed writing.

Really Max had begun to suspect that their camp-mate must be writing a story, founded on that strange cabin, with its lichen-covered walls, and the roof that seemed to be sprouting green grass with the moss.

One glance he took at the brave heading that began the page. The title was quite enough for Max. With a broad grin he quietly laid it down, gave the industrious writer one amused look, and walked away again, without Bandy-legs knowing of the visit.

And no wonder Max felt amused, for what he had seen spread across that page, in letters that were heavily underscored, was this wonderful title:

"Programme for meals during six more days to be spent on Catamount Island!"

Bandy-legs was trying to forget all his troubles by laying out the *menu* for the balance of their week.

It was about an hour before sundown that Steve came hurriedly into camp. he carried a pretty good mess of fish, which attested to the fact that, impatient as he was in nearly everything else, at the same time he seemed to be a pretty fair waiter when holding a rod and reel in his hand. Perhaps the constant expectation of a bite kept him in decent humor.

But now Max saw that he was considerably excited.

"What ails you, Steve?" asked Owen, who also detected some unusual signs of disgust about the returned fisherman; "did the biggest get away, like it always does? Well, we'll believe you, never fear; especially if he yanked your hook off, and broke your line in the bargain. How big do you think he was, Steve?"

"That old gag don't work this time, Owen," remarked the other, as he deposited his catch on the ground, to be admired by Bandy-legs immediately. "I'm. wanting to kick myself for being silly, that's all"

"Oh, well, I wouldn't bother about that," Max put in, kindly. "There are four of us here, and we ought to be able to do the business to suit you. When shall we begin operations, Steve?"

But even then Steve did not lose his look of disappointment.

"To think that I sat there all that time," he remarked, "and never once remembered that bully field glass we've got along."

At this remark Max realized that the distress of their chum could not be based on anything connected with his fishing experience.

"Hello!" he exclaimed; "now you've got us guessing, all right, Steve. You must have seen something or other, I reckon. Out with it, please."

"Well, I did," replied the other, quickly. "You see, I was sitting there, waiting for an old buster of a bass I'd got a glimpse of several times to come up and get hold of my hook, when I happened to look across to the shore at just the widest part, where it's far away. And right off I discovered that it had been something moving that caught my eye as it were."

"A panther!" gasped Bandy-legs, involuntarily letting his hand creep down to his left ankle, where those scratches still proved the truth of his story that something, the nature of which was unknown, had grabbed him on the preceding night.

"Rats!" scoffed Steve, loftily. "Panthers don't prowl around in the daytime—that is, not very much. It was a human being I saw; and then a second appeared right at his elbow. They seemed to be mighty much interested in this here island, too; for the first one pointed across, and up and down, like he was trying to explain how a swimmer might get over."

"Goodness gracious! Steve, were they men or boys!" demanded Bandy-legs.

"Now I know you're thinking about Herb Benson; or it might be that tricky Ted Shafter," remarked Steve.

"Well, didn't we kinder half 'spect we'd have a visit from one or t'other of them crowds, p'r'aps both?" demanded Bandy-legs, with an injured air.

"All right; but these fellows didn't look like either lot. Then again, I'm right sure I saw the sun, away down in the west you see, shining from something bright. Couldn't make it out first, and then all of a sudden it broke in on me that they had a pair of field glasses, and must be examining this island. That made me remember our own pair, and I hurried to get back off that log I was straddling; but before I'd been able to make the shore, hang the luck, they'd gone."

"Perhaps they saw you, and wanted to keep out of sight?" suggested Max.

"That's just what they must 'a' done," admitted Steve. "But where's the bally old glasses, fellows? I might lie around, and keep tabs on that shore for a spell. Who knows but what they might show up again; and I'm curious to learn just who they can be."

Max quickly vanished inside the tent, and came out with the desired object in his hand.

"Before you go, Steve, tell us whether they looked like men or boys?" he asked, handing the field glasses over.

"Well, I couldn't see as good as I wanted," was the hesitating reply; "but 'peared to me they were men, all right. And they seemed to be dressed in gray homespun, too, like some of the farmers around here wear."

"Oh, perhaps after all it may have been a couple of young farmers taking a day off, hunting woodcock along the river. This is the time of year for the first brood to be big enough for shooting. The law opens for a short spell, and then it's on again till fall," Owen remarked, with his knowledge of such things, gleaned from much reading.

"They didn't seem to have any guns that I saw," observed Steve, doggedly, as he hurried away.

This gave the others something to talk about until the shades of evening began to gather around them. Who these two men could be, and just *why* they seemed to take such an interest in Catamount

Island, were questions that the boys debated from all sides. Even Bandy-legs seemed to be stirred up, and made all sorts of ridiculous suggestions.

Steve came in finally. It only required one look at his disappointed face to tell that he had not met with any success in his latest mission. Even the delightful odor of his freshly caught bass, cooking in the frying pan over the fire, failed to make Steve look happier. He did hate to be beaten in anything he undertook.

"Nothing doing, Steve?" questioned Bandy-legs; for there is a saying to the effect that "babes and fools rush in where brave men hesitate to tread"; which, however, must not be taken to mean that Bandy-legs belonged to either class, although he failed to approach a subject with tact.

"Naw!" snapped Steve, as he hung the case containing the glasses up in its accustomed place inside the tent.

A few minutes later, finding that no one bothered him for information, Steve, who was really brimming over with a desire to argue the matter with his comrades, opened the subject himself.

"Say, now, Max, you don't suppose that it could have been any of them fellows, do you?" he asked.

Max, who was adjusting the coffee pot nicely on the slender iron bars that formed what he was accustomed to call his "cooking stove," these four resting on solid foundation of stones on either side of the hot little fire, turned his head when Steve addressed him particularly.

"Which way did they seem to go when they left?" he asked, slowly, as though the answer might have a good deal to do with his opinion.

"Up the river," replied Steve, promptly.

"Well, then, I don't believe it could have been any of the boys," was what Max went on to state; "and I'll tell you several reasons for saying that. In the first place there would have been three if it was the Ted Shafter crowd; and perhaps more if Herb had come up here to see whether we were really camping on Catamount Island."

"Right you are, Max," remarked Owen, who was listening carefully.

"Then again, what would they be doing away up here so late in the day?" the other continued. "Why, it's miles and miles by road back to town. Even by the river in a boat they couldn't make it short of two hours; and traveling at night along the rapid Big Sunflower would be a ticklish job that I wouldn't like to tackle. Last of all, why go on *up* the river? If they came in a boat, it would have to be down below us, you know, boys."

There was no dissenting voice raised against this line of argument on the part of Max. And when they sat down to eat their supper the talk was wholly confined to the subject of the two mysterious men. Who were they, and why did they seem to be so greatly interested in Catamount Island? And when Steve made a move that must have attracted their attention, why had they bolted so hastily?

Again did all manner of surmises float to the surface. Bandy-legs was beginning to show signs of nervousness once more. Possibly the coming of darkness had much to do with his condition, for he shuddered every time he felt that scratched ankle give him a twinge. For Bandy-legs feared that he was a marked person; and that if the dreaded occupant of the strange cabin chose to pay them another visit before dawn, he would be the one picked out for trouble.

He seemed uneasy about supper, and wandered down to where the four canoes lay upon the sandy strip, as though the desire to again examine that plugged hole in the bottom of his cedar craft had seized upon him.

Those near the fire were paying little attention to Bandy-legs, for they happened just then to have started an argument along some line, and Steve was warmly defending his radical views.

And when they heard Bandy-legs give utterance to a shrill whoop they scrambled to their feet, half expecting to find that some fearful shape had darted out from the surrounding forest, and was carrying their chum away.

CHAPTER X.

THE BUILDER OF THE STRANGE CABIN.

"What is it, Bandy-legs?" shouted Steve, who, in spite of his constant quarreling with the other, felt a great amount of affection for him.

He had pounced down upon the ax, which happened to be lying close by, and this he flourished around his head as he started to meet the figure that was scrambling up the little bank above the beach.

"Whoo, somethin' jumped at me!" replied the startled boy, panting for breath; for he had fallen at least twice, in his haste to rejoin his campmates near the blazing fire.

Max took hold of him as he came up, and started to ask questions. Perhaps he already began to suspect that Bandy-legs was allowing his fears to run away with his judgment. There was such a thing as being frightened at one's own shadow.

"Are you sure you saw something, Bandy-legs?" he asked.

"Course I am," came the reply.

"And it wasn't your shadow this time?" Max continued.

Now, had Steve put It in exactly the same way, the boy would have shown immediate indignation; but he seemed to understand that Max meant every word, and was not simply trying to tease him. So he replied in like good faith.

"It sure wasn't, Max. Why, just when I was goin' to bend down over my canoe, to see how things looked inside, it gave a nasty little spit straight in my face, and went whirling over the side. And, Max, it had a tail as big as a broom, honest it did."

"Oh, that means it must have been a 'coon," remarked Max, beginning to laugh.

"But what would a measly old raccoon want in my canoe?" demanded Bandy-legs. "If he just had to come snoopin' around, why couldn't the critter pick out a boat belongin' to somebody else? Seems like everything has a spite against just me."

"Well, of course, I can't tell you that," remarked Max. "If you want to know you'll have to ask the 'coon. Perhaps you may have dropped a small piece of food in your boat; and as he came prowling around, not very much afraid of us here, he got track of the same, and was hunting for it when you had to disturb him."

"I don't wonder he sniffed in your face when you poked your head in there," declared Steve. "Nobody likes to be bothered when they're eating. Just try taking a bone away from a hungry dog or cat, once, and see. He thought you a busybody, that's what, Bandy-legs. But he's gone now, if so be you want to investigate, and find out whether the 'coon chawed another hole in your canoe."

But Bandy-legs only threw himself down by the fire.

His air was that of one who was determined not to be easily lured away from so comfortable a place until it was time to go to bed. They could see that Bandy-legs was really becoming quite worked up over the queer way a fickle fortune seemed to be showering little adventures on his shoulders, while the rest went scot free.

"Ain't we goin' to stand guard to-night, fellers?" he asked later on; showing how the subject stuck in his mind.

"Guard over what?" asked Steve.

"Why, that critter is bent on stealing every bit of our grub, and we ought to do everything we can to break up his game," Bandy-legs affirmed, in a firm way that was rather new to him.

"As how?" further questioned Steve; while the others listened as if interested.

"Well, s'pose Max here laid out a plan that would give every feller two hours on the watch," pursued Bandy-legs, proudly, as though he had conjured up this beautiful little scheme all by himself, while sitting there staring into the fire. "If I had that shotgun in my hands, I'd just like to see anybody, or anything, sneak in on us, and steal as much as an egg."

"I guess you would be a pretty dangerous customer, with a loaded gun in your hands, the way you feel right now," remarked Max, seriously. "Come, you mustn't think so much about it, Bandy-legs. Leave it to us, and we'll try and fix it all right."

"But I've got an idea of a trap in my mind I'd like to try out," protested the other, eagerly.

"That's all right," laughed Max, "so long as you don't fall into it yourself, and get us all up in the middle of the night. You must promise not to creep out at any time, to see if there's anything in it."

"Oh, you'll know it, all right, if it does ketch game," grinned Bandy-legs. "You see, I was readin' just last week about a crocodile hunter away off in Africa; and he used to set his traps about like the way I'm goin' to do mine now."

"Go on and tell us about it, please?" asked Owen, always interested.

"I've known farmers' boys to make the same sort of snare to grab rabbits in the winter time," Bandy-legs went on, being a most accommodating boy, especially when he had anything to tell about his own doings. "You find a nice stout hickory sapling of the right kind, and strip it of all the branches. Then you bend it over, and fasten it to a crotched stick you've pounded hard in the ground. The end of the sapling has a stout cord tied to it, and this is made in the shape of a noose. The bait is put in this, and bunny gets his leg caught in the loop, which tightens, so he tugs to get away. Then up goes the sapling, when the trigger is sprung, and the game hangs there, kicking in the air."

"Fine!" remarked Steve, admiringly; "and the chances are just two to one, old fellow, that if you set a trap like that for a visitor, you'll be the first to fall into it."

"Oh, say, can't you let a feller get up even a little thing like that without throwing cold water on him?" complained Bandy-legs, in a grieved tone. "Max, don't you think it'd work, if I tried it?"

"It might," came the reply; "and perhaps there wouldn't be any harm done trying. It's a pretty smart scheme, let me tell you, Bandy-legs. And if we heard a yell, and crawled out to see the thief hanging there, all the credit would be yours."

That settled it. Words of praise from so good an authority as Max would brush away all the sarcastic remarks Steve could think up. So Bandy-legs, with a look of triumph at his opponent, picked up the ax and sauntered off again. But he was very careful to keep within the magical circle of light cast by the blazing camp fire.

They heard him chopping away presently.

"Found the very hickory you wanted, have you?" called out Max.

"Just suits the bill, O. K.," replied the busy one.

After a little he came back for a piece of the rope.

"Don't take more than you need," Owen remarked. "Before we leave here that rope may come in handy. You never can tell."

"Yes," said Steve, with grim humor; "and there's a mighty convenient limb sticking out nearly straight and horizontal from that tree over yonder. If we happened to be out West now instead of ten miles from Carson, the chances are they'd know what that same limb was meant for."

"Oh, come, none of that stuff," Max protested, for he saw that Bandy-legs frowned and looked a trifle unwilling to go away from the circle again. "This is a peaceful community, and they never use ropes that way around here."

Ten minutes later and they heard a sudden snap, accompanied by certain pawing sounds, and a great grunting. Hurrying over to where the trap setter had been hard at work they found him with his hands on the ground, and one leg held high up in the air by the noose he had made of the rope.

Despite the efforts of Bandy-legs, he seemed unable to reach the rope, and only for the prompt assistance of his chums he might have had a serious time of it. Of course Steve laughed as if he would have a fit, even while the others were taking the unfortunate trapper down.

"Works all right, don't it, Bandy-legs?" he demanded. "When they got a new play that they want to try out in some small city away from New York, they say they're trying it on the dog first. And looks like you—"

"Shut up!" roared Bandy-legs, turning on his tormentor. "I wanted to see if it would go off, that's all."

"Well, it did!" remarked Steve, dryly.

"And now I'm goin' to set it for fair," returned the other, who seemed to be so well pleased with the result of his labors that he could even take Steve's chaffing with some degree of good humor.

They left him there, all but Max, who stayed to render any assistance the ardent trapper might need. For Max had an idea that perhaps the trap might play a part in the discovery of the unknown thief, should he take a notion to pay the camp another visit that night.

Then they all sat around the blaze and chatted once more.

"Does anybody know the history of this island, and who ever lived here?" asked Max. "That cabin must have been built a good many years ago, I'd think, judging from the looks of it."

"Say, I was thinkin' about that same thing this afternoon, when sittin' on that log fishing," spoke up Steve.

"Then you remembered something about it, did you?" asked Owen.

"That's what I did," came the ready response. "But it was a long time ago, and I must 'a' been only a little kid then, because I don't seem to just recollect the whole story."

"Tell us what you do remember, Steve?" suggested Max.

"Yes," continued Bandy-legs, "I'd give a lot to know whoever was silly enough to want to live on this wild-looking old island, where in the spring they say the flood sometimes nearly covers everything. You c'n see the drift hanging to the butts of some of the trees right now, and all pointin' downstream."

"Good for you, Bandy-legs!" exclaimed the pleased Max; "I never thought you'd notice such things. Owen and myself were talking about it; but when you get to paying attention to such small matters it shows that you're just bound to make a good woodsman some fine day."

"You bet I am," confided the other, cheerfully, his eyes glistening with pleasure at hearing one he respected so highly as Max Hastings hand out praise in this manner.

"Go on, Steve, tell us what you know," Owen observed, encouragingly.

"Well, I just happened to hear my dad talkin' with another gentleman once, and it was about this same island up here. They called it Catamount then, like they do right now. He said that a long time before, a man by the name of Wesley Coombs had bought the place for a song from the owners, and with his wife and baby here, started to clear the timber off. So you see 'twas him that put up the queer little old cabin here. He thought he could have a great home of it in time."

"Yes, I saw a number of big trees that must have been felled with the ax years ago," Max remarked at this point; "and I was wondering about it."

"W-w-what happened to W-w-wesley C-c-combs?" asked Toby.

"It was a mighty sad thing, my dad said," Steve went on, a tremor in his own voice, for Steve was tender-hearted after his fashion; "you see, the first winter he was here he made quite a heap of money trappin' furs, and fishing through the ice for pickerel that he sold in town. Then in the spring the floods came and the whole little family was wiped out; though the cabin, bein' built so strong, held out against the freshet, and it has ever since, too."

"All drowned, Wesley Coombs, his wife, and his baby, too; that's a tough story of the old island you're giving us, Steve," remarked Owen.

"Well, they said as how the man was saved, but he was stark starin' mad; and my dad said he died later on. I never could get that story out of my bead for a long time. It gave me a bad feeling this afternoon when I remembered the same, and I thought of that little cabin once being a happy home."

"Gee! I hope one of them same floods don't take a notion to swoop down this way while we're camped on Catamount Island!" declared Bandy-legs.

"Oh, well, we'd get home in a hurry if it did," remarked Steve, indifferently. "You know, they said our canoes couldn't sink, because they've got air tanks fitted away up in the bow and back in the stern. All we'd have to do would be to lash ourselves to 'em with pieces of that rope, and float along till we got opposite Carson, when we'd yell for help. Yes, Owen was right; that rope might come in handy one way or another, yet."

"For shame, Steve," called out Max; "trying to mike Bandy-legs nervous again. There never was a flood at this time of year, take my word for it. But we'll try and make ourselves as secure as we can, with our canoes in the bargain; because, if those Shafters did take it into their heads to raid us tonight, we want to be ready for them."

And it was with that idea in mind that the campers busied themselves for half an hour or so before the time they had set for crawling under their blankets, and "wooing the moose," as Bandy-legs put it, meaning to cast a sly reflection on the well-known habit Steve had of snoring in his sleep when lying on his back.

CHAPTER XI.

WHAT HAPPENED ON THE SECOND NIGHT.

"Owen, Owen, wake up!"

When Bandy-legs dug his elbow into the side of his sleeping chum, and whispered these words in his ear, naturally enough the said Owen could not help but awaken.

"What ails you?" he asked sleepily; and even Steve stirred as though the sound of their voices had aroused him.

"My trap's sprung!" was the rather surprising information Bandy-legs vouchsafed in return.

"The dickens you say!" exclaimed Owen, suddenly sitting up in the darkness. "Now, how d'ye know that fact? Did anything give a yelp?"

"No," continued the other, eagerly; "but you see, Owen, before I went to sleep I had Max tie a string to my leg and the other end to that loop. It was fixed under the root of a tree; and if the trap went off, why, don't you see, the string'd give me just a sweet little yank, like it wanted to tell me to come around and take my game out."

"And did you feel that same yank?" demanded Steve, sitting up suddenly.

"Right now, before I woke Owen up. Oh, it was a sure enough jerk, all right! What'll we do about it?" demanded Bandy-legs.

"Let's crawl out and see what happened," remarked Owen, setting his actions to correspond with his words, and being followed by his two companions.

"What is it?"

That was Max speaking, and they could see his head poked out from the partly open flap of the smaller tent. Evidently he must have been awake at the time, or else the sound of murmuring voices aroused him; for Max always declared that he was a very light sleeper.

"Bandy-legs here says his trap is sprung," remarked Owen. "He tells us you fixed a string to his leg and the other end to the loop. Well, that just gave him word something had happened."

"We'll soon find out," was all Max remarked, as he proceeded to crawl all the way out of his tent.

Stepping over he picked up the lantern, and a match that had been left handily near by. And so it took but a fraction of a minute for them to possess a light that would answer all purposes.

The four of them then approached the place where Bandy-legs had set his wonderful snare, which he had tested so well himself to start with.

"Huh! I don't see anybody swinging around here!" remarked the always skeptical Steve.

"Neither do I," added Owen, in a tone of disappointment.

"But see, fellers, the old trap, she's gone off!" exclaimed Bandy-legs, in a thrilling tone. "Didn't I tell you I felt a pull that woke me up? It worked, just you bet it did, now."

The hickory sapling was indeed standing up almost straight, with the loop dangling part way down; but the snare was devoid of any victim.

Max looked around as best he could with such a poor light.

"I don't see the first sign of any tracks here," he remarked.

"Shucks, the chances are Bandy-legs might have kicked in the night, and that was enough to set the loop free!" Steve declared.

"He couldn't do that," answered Max; "I fixed that string in such a way there was no danger of it happening. But I rather think some fox in hunting around set the thing off, but didn't get caught in the spread loop. It was set for bigger game, you remember, boys."

"Well, I'm going back to my blanket again," said Owen. "It feels chilly out here, and there's no use staying."

Even Bandy-legs seemed to have lost all faith in his wonderful snare; for he declined to stay long enough to put it in working order again. Twice now it had gone off, and there could be no telling what the third result might be if he ventured to try it again, which he would not.

There was no further alarm, and at dawn the boys came piling out of their tents. The weather seemed to have grown a bit sultry, so Max remarked that perhaps a dip in the water of the Big Sunflower might not feel out of the way.

So they had a happy little time of it, splashing each other, and carrying on as any five carefree lads might be expected to; until all of them decided they had had enough, when dressing was the next thing on the programme.

Bandy-legs was the first to finish. The fire was burning briskly, and a nice red bed of embers between the side stones invited the attention of the cook of the morning, namely himself.

"Say, where'd you hang that half of a ham, Owen?" he asked, after what seemed a vain search.

"Just where we always kept it," was the reply; "suspended from that limb of the oak over—well, did anybody change it around or take it inside the tent?" and Owen looked his surprise, when the others all shook their heads in the negative.

"It's gone!" cried Bandy-legs, looking very unhappy; "our nice ham's been hooked!"

A rush was made for the oak tree in question.

"There's the twine I hung it up by, dangling from the limb right now," declared Owen, pointing.

"But show me the ham, will you?" asked Bandy-legs. "We can't make a decent breakfast off string that's only got a ham flavor, can we?"

"Why, it must have been full six feet up from the ground," remarked Steve, for the benefit of Bandy-legs; "I never thought before a panther could leap *that* high!"

"Oh, gracious!" began Bandy-legs; and then, seeing the look on Steve's face, he understood that the other was only baiting him for a fall: whereupon he shut his jaws hard together, and determined not to be taken in.

Max, of course, was already looking for signs. It was his opinion that few things could happen without there being evident traces left behind, if only one knew how to find them.

"Here's a track, fellows; and it looks like the same we saw before!" he called out, presently, as he bent over eagerly.

"It sure does," admitted Owen.

"Right under where our lovely ham hung, too," wailed Bandy-legs.

"All he had to do was to reach up and grab it," commented Owen.

Toby did not say anything, but went through a pantomime movement as of a man taking possession of some object dangling there from the limb.

"I wish now we'd taken it in our tent, when Max complained that the ham smell made it unpleasant in his own," Bandy-legs went on.

"There was a man once who actually locked the door of his stable after his horse was took," Steve ventured; at which Max laughed.

"Well, it does look like we'd have to go without ham for a while, boys; but after all, it was only a half. Think how bad we'd feel if it was a whole one. And whoever took it must have been pretty hungry in the bargain. He's been living on partridges right along, when he could find any in his snares. The rest of the time he went without a bite, seems like."

"But, Max, who is he?" asked Steve; at which the other shrugged his shoulders.

"Ask me something easy, boys," he replied. "I've never seen him even once, like Herb and his chums did, when they tried to sleep in that queer old cabin. But you see, we've got his footprints right here in the dirt. They ought to tell us something, perhaps."

"But, Max, footprints can't talk, can they?" demanded Bandy-legs,

"Always, in their own language," was the ready reply. "You have to study that a while though, before you can understand what they say."

"Oh, yes, I'm on to you now, Max," cried the other, triumphantly; "you mean that you can tell it was a man by the size of the prints; ain't that it?"

"One of many things," answered Max. "Now, this seems to have been a pretty hefty sort of fellow, because the marks are big. It is a common shoe, too, just like the men make and wear in the prisons and public institutions."

Bandy-legs fairly gasped for breath at hearing this remark. To his mind it seemed to imply that the mysterious dweller of the strange cabin on Catamount Island must be an escaped convict, a desperate ruffian, who might take a notion to murder them all in their sleep.

"And we've still got five more nights to stay here!" he groaned, as though with that new intelligence the very last hope he was cherishing of ever being able to see his folks again vanished like a puff of smoke in the wind.

"Say, that makes me think of something," Steve broke out just then.

"About what?" asked Max, turning from his examination of the plain footprint at the place where the unknown visitor had stood when reaching up for the tempting half of a smoked ham.

"Those two men," the other went on to say.

"What about 'em?" asked Owen.

"I said they wore gray homespun clothes, didn't I, just like the farmers, plenty of 'em, have around these diggings? Well, I've changed my mind, boys. It just broke in on me that I saw somethin' flash every time they moved this way and that. No, it wasn't the field glasses either; but somethin' about their clothes. Brass buttons, I reckon, boys! Them men might 'a' been wardens from the penitentiary, lookin' for a prisoner that escaped some time ago!"

Steve drew himself up proudly, as though conscious of the fact that he had hit upon a very plausible explanation of the mystery. Max was evidently thinking it over, for his face seemed serious enough, to be sure.

"That doesn't sound so much out of the way, Steve," he admitted. "Fact is, it may be the very thing. Some of these guards have gray uniforms, I believe; and they put brass buttons on the same, just to make them look official-like. Yes, they wanted to get over here, and didn't have a boat. Perhaps they've gone up river to get one, and cross to the island. They might try it to-day; and then again perhaps they'd wait for another night, for fear of frightening him away, and losing him somehow if he jumped into the river."

"What a peck of trouble we've sure struck since we took on that dare," Owen remarked, just then.

"Yes," added Bandy-legs, with a sad look, "and the end ain't come along yet, by a big sight."

Of course they had plenty of other things to supply the lack of ham for breakfast. Max even went to the trouble of making some flapjacks, just to take away the bitter disappointment Bandy-legs seemed to feel over the disappearance of the joint. And all of them united in declaring that they did not care how soon he had the same notion again, the cakes were so fine.

The day was very warm, and having been reminded that the Big Sunflower River was capable of assuming the dimensions of a flood upon certain occasions, nervous Bandy-legs turned one eye upward from time to time, as though trying to figure out whether they might expect a cloudburst of some sort, should a storm drop in upon them.

Steve joked him more than a little about his new fears.

"Got your tree all picked out, have you, Bandy-legs?" he would remark in his bantering way. "Be sure and tie your canoe to the lower limb, so it'll stay by you. And feel a little pity, won't you, please, for the other poor fellers who go ridin' down the raging flood, hangin' on to the bottom of their boats? Oh, it's a wise guy you show yourself, old boy. They don't ketch you asleep, do they? Weasels ain't in it with Bandy-legs, boys. You see from the way he looks at that oak yonder, that's his choice, when she comes bowling along here."

Max had some little scheme of his own on his mind. He did not even take his cousin into his confidence; but along after lunch he picked up the gun, and, remarking that he might go for a little walk along the shore, left them wondering.

They knew Max well enough to feel pretty certain he must have something "hatching," as Steve put it; and all sorts of guesses were indulged in during his absence.

Although the four boys left in camp amused themselves in a variety of ways, even fishing with fair success, as Steve had done on the preceding day, time hung heavy on their hands that afternoon. It seemed as though the sun would never draw near the line of far-away hills that marked the western horizon.

More than a few times Owen would look up, as some slight sound caught his ear. He was listening for the report of the gun Max carried; but as the minutes turned into hours, and nothing was heard, Owen began to grow anxious.

He had almost reached the point of proposing that they give a halloo, and if no reply came, start out to look for the absent chum, when a moving figure up the shore caught his attention, and presently it developed into Max.

"See anything of the convict?" asked Steve, upon whom that idea seemed to have taken a decided hold.

Max shook his head in the negative.

"Have you been up to that cabin again?" asked Owen, suspiciously.

"I suppose I might as well tell you that I've laid a little plan that, if it only turns out well, may bag the unknown visitor we had last night," Max confessed. "You see, when we were up there the other day, I noticed that old as it was, the cabin was as strong as anything. If a fellow could only slip up, and shoot a bar across the door in any way after *some one* went inside, it'd be dollars to doughnuts he'd find the chap there in the morning."

"And when would you do all this fine slipping-up business?" asked Steve.

"I'm going there again to-night," Max continued, positively; "and lie around to see what happens. And none of you need say a single word, because you don't come along with me. When I've managed to secure that door as I've arranged for, it'll be time enough to let you know about it. Forget it now, boys; and let's talk about supper."

Bandy-legs stared hard at Max, as though he could not believe his ears. That anyone would dare venture all the way up to that strange cabin in the darkness of the night, and even try and capture the desperate ruffian whom they now believed to be an escaped convict, amazed him.

Sure enough, that night, about the time the boys under ordinary conditions would be thinking of seeking their blankets, Max quietly took his gun and vanished from the sight of his chums.

He had taken particular note of every step of the route along the bank with this night journey in view. And he felt now that he could silently make his way along without anything bordering upon an accident. Had any of the others been with him a clumsy mis-step was apt to create trouble; and Bandy-legs in particular was always getting into a mess.

Max had reached a point about halfway up the shore of Catamount Island when he suddenly stopped short and crouched low. Surely that was the low sound of voices coming to his ear. And he immediately recognized the fact that the murmur must be carried across the water, which is such a splendid conveyer of sounds.

Then some persons must be coming off from the shore in a boat! His mind went back to what Steve had seen of the two men in gray uniforms. Were they about to land on the island now, bent upon recapturing the desperate man who was hiding there.

Max had just about come to this decision when he had occasion to alter his views of the matter. He heard a peculiar little cough, which struck him as mighty familiar. Their old enemy, Ted Shafter, had an odd way of making such a sound; and there were those who said it was caused by smoking so many cigarettes. Did this cigarette cough mean that Ted and his two cronies were coming to play a practical joke on the campers of Catamount Island?

CHAPTER XII.

A BOLD PLAN.

"Hold on, fellers! Let's get a line on what this rotten old shore looks like," Max plainly heard Ted Shafter say, in a low tone.

The oars continued to dip in the water, for unless this were done continually the swift current would carry the boat downstream rapidly enough.

Looking closely at the point from whence the sound proceeded Max believed he could make out an object that seemed darker than the surroundings. This then must be the boat in which the three boys had pulled all the way up from Carson; a job not to be sneered at, considering the weight of the craft, and the strength of the current.

"Hang the luck, Ted, I can't see anything but just a solid blur," remarked another of the occupants of the boat; and Max knew that it was Shack Beggs, whose father was an engineer in one of the works at Carson, who made this disgusted remark.

"I can see trees, and I think some rocks," said a third one, undoubtedly Amiel Toots; for he had a soft oily voice, just as Amiel was a soft oily boy, treacherous by nature, and only faithful to Ted because he really feared the big bully.

"That accounts for the whole bunch of them," Max was saying to himself, and at the same time endeavoring to figure out how he could give the three rowdies a scare that would send them flying down the river, not to come back again.

Max thought he saw a way of accomplishing this much-to-be-desired end. He had in his pocket several flashlight powders that he had intended using in the line of photography, if the occasion ever arose for trying to take a picture during the period of darkness. With them he also carried a clever little arrangement fashioned after the style of a pistol, whereby with a pressure of one finger the flash could be brought about.

There, they were talking again, after all of them had been trying their hardest to make out the conformation of the shore near which they were at the time.

"Reckon yuh must move in a little closer, Ted, if so be yuh 'spect us tuh see just where tuh land," Shack remarked.

"Don't you think we ought to go a little slow about landing?" remarked Amiel, who evidently had certain fears of his own, which same caused his soft oily voice to quiver painfully.

"Aw! what's the matter with you?" grated Ted, savagely. "Just acause them fellers go to talkin' 'bout ghosts and all that stuff, you're afraid, that's what! Sho! didn't we see Max Hastings and his crowd there on the foot of the plagued island? If they could stay here two nights a'ready, what's a-goin' to hurt us inside of only one hour, tell me that, hey?"

When Max heard this he came near chuckling. It seemed to answer the question he had been asking himself; for he wondered whether these fellows could have heard about the scare Herb and his friends received some little time ago, when they tried to stop on the island over night.

Apparently, then, they had, and the fact had even made a strong impression on the weakest one of the lot, Amiel Toots. And Max was not so sure about the others being very far removed from fear in connection with that same subject, much as they made out to show courage.

"It's going to work all right, see if it don't," Max whispered to himself, as he began to make ready to start things moving.

First of all he wanted to screen his own body completely from sight; for when the sudden vivid flash came it would disclose every little object around for a radius of many feet. This was easily accomplished. A convenient tree trunk offered a friendly asylum; and back of this he might hide, so that no one could see him, from the river side at least.

First of all he gave a very dismal groan. Max was not up in matters pertaining to ghosts in general, and could only make a guess at emitting the proper kind of sound; but really it did seem quite "shivery," even to the boy responsible for making it.

"Glory be! What was that?" he heard Amiel ask, instantly.

Utter silence followed, and apparently everyone in the boat was listening with might and main for a repetition of the groan. Max thought it would be a pity to disappoint those fellows. They had come so *very* far just to have some fun; and if they were now compelled to go all the way back to Carson without ever having the least amusement, think of the trouble they had taken for nothing! And after all, it was so easy to give them good measure, brimming full, and running over. So he groaned three times in rapid succession, just as if the troubled spirit might be getting impatient.

He heard exclamations of renewed alarm from the pitch darkness; for clouds shut out what little light might have come from the heavens above.

"Let's get out of this, boys!" Ted was heard to say.

"Hurry, hurry! I thought I saw something moving right then! Be quick, fellows!" Amiel Toots exclaimed, in thick accents, as though his fright had become such as to seriously interfere with the working of his vocal cords.

Max waited no longer. He knew that the boat, drifting down with the current, was now exactly opposite to him. He heard the splash of the oars striking the water; although in their haste and clumsiness the three Carson boys were in danger of upsetting their craft while trying to turn so quickly.

Max pressed the trigger of his little flashlight pistol. Instantly a dazzling light sprang forth, blinding the eyes of the three in the boat just as if they had met with a bolt of descending lightning.

Then it was gone, as quick as that, leaving the darkness of the night more noticeable than before. Max was satisfied with his work. He heard cries of horror break forth from Ted Shafter and his two cronies. Amiel Toots even started to crying like a big baby, he was so badly frightened; while the others tugged at the oars desperately, in the endeavor to turn the boat, so as to head downstream.

And when they did finally get started, the way they tugged at those ashen blades was enough to win almost any race.

"Good-by, Ted and Company!" said Max, not out loud, but to himself in a low tone; for he did not want to lessen the fear that had gripped those three fellows.

He could hear the sound of the oars working furiously in the rowlocks long after the fugitives must have passed the lower end of the island. Of course the rest of the campers would catch the sounds that had welled forth, and feel curious about them; but between the four they ought to be able to figure out what it meant. And as the fact of his possessing the flashlight powders was known, they must realize that he, Max, was at the bottom of the whole affair.

As Max continued his forward progress he was trying to understand what Ted and his friends had meant to do. They knew, of course, how the campers expected to stay there on Catamount Island for a whole week; and the temptation to try and play a mean trick on Max and his chums had finally moved them to get a boat, and row all the way up here.

No doubt they had arrived in the vicinity of the island at some time during the afternoon; but unwilling to show themselves, lest their intentions be thwarted, they had waited down around the next bend until darkness came along to conceal their movements.

Just what they expected to do no one ever knew; but such mean tricks were always cropping up in the minds of the trio, that even the setting adrift of all the canoes, thus compelling the campers to swim ashore, and foot it all the way back to Carson, would not be anything unusual for them.

However, there need be little fear that those three frightened boys would ever make a second attempt to land on Catamount Island, especially during the night time. So far as they were concerned, the campers might now rest easy; and even Bandy-legs, when he heard the facts, could draw a relieved breath.

Max now tried to forget all about the recent little adventure, and fix his whole mind on what lay ahead of him. He had started out on what seemed rather a risky errand, if, as they suspected, the occupant of the strange cabin was really a desperate escaped convict. Still, Max was a brave lad; and having once conceived this little plan of campaign, he could not force himself to give it up, just because it carried a spice of danger.

He knew that at a certain point, which he had marked, he must leave the shore of the island, and turn aside. Through dense shrubbery then his course lay; but he had marked it well in his mind, so that he could follow it faithfully, even in pitch darkness. And it was only a little way, after all, before he would come upon the strange cabin with the green roof and lichen-covered side logs.

Several times he stopped to listen, but heard no suspicious sound. Once a small animal of some sort started off nearly under his feet, and gave the boy a shock; but nevertheless he did not turn back. Having made his mind up on a certain matter, it would have to be something more than that to make him change his plans.

Before quitting camp he had asked his chums to leave something in the line of food, where it could be easily found by a roving man, while out of the reach of foxes, 'coons, and 'possums. This he meant to be in the shape of a bait. If the half-starved marooned convict once got it in his clutch he would undoubtedly make straight for the cabin retreat, there to devour his prize. And it was while the unknown party was engaged in this delightful task that Max expected to slip up and fasten the door by means of the arrangement he had fixed that afternoon, a very simple affair, too, as it turned out.

Now he could just distinguish the dark blur ahead of him, which he knew must be made by the cabin itself. As the trees were not quite so dense overhead in this spot, for once upon a time, many years ago, poor Wesley Coombs had started to clear around his then newly made log cabin, Max was soon able to make out the partly open door, just as he had found, and also left it, so as not to excite the suspicions of his intended victim.

Then he settled down to watch, hoping that if the man were waiting for a chance to steal more food, he would soon find an opportunity, and come hurrying back to dispose of it as before. For Max had found the bone of their ham, picked clean, in the shack that afternoon when he visited it; though there had been no sign of any human being around at the time, the man evidently only sleeping under that old but stout roof.

CHAPTER XIII.

UNSEEN PERILS THAT HOVERED NEAR.

Once Max had crept softly up to the side of the cabin and listened, with all his senses on the alert. If the unknown were asleep within, he surely must have betrayed the fact by his labored breathing.

No sound, however slight, came to the alert ears of the boy from inside the strange cabin; and from this fact he felt pretty positive that it must be entirely empty at the time.

After that he moved back again and took up his old station, where the undergrowth would shelter him. He had picked out the place in the daylight, and made sure it was not in the path one would naturally take when coming from the lower end of the island. When settling this matter Max had in mind the unpleasant nature of the meeting should the other stumble upon him as he hid there waiting.

How slowly the minutes passed! To kill the time he began counting, as though in imagination he could see the great pendulum of the grandfather clock that stood in the hall at home, why even a minute seemed enormously long, and five of them an eternity.

Then he allowed his mind to roam back again to the camp, where his four chums were at that minute. He was trying to picture the coming of the escaped convict in his striped suit, creeping up like a stealthy tiger, and quickly discovering the food that had been left there as a bait.

How eagerly would he pounce upon it, and then head back to the vicinity of the lonely cabin, around which clung such sad memories of that tragedy of the long ago, when the waters came up in the night, and took the whole Coombs family off to their death.

Once Max felt his nerves thrill with expectancy, as he caught a movement close by. His hands involuntarily tightened on the stock of the gun he carried, not to use upon the convict, but as a measure of precaution.

Listening intently, he felt sure that he could detect a slight creeping sound, as if some one, or some *thing*, were stealthily approaching the spot where he crouched, and held his very breath with suspense.

Surely this could not be a man making his way along. Such a burly figure must make more noise than now reached him. Only a sleek animal could pass from log to log with but a faint pat of feet; or it might be the brushing of the bushes in its progress toward him.

But it was no small raccoon or mink that was slowly approaching, as though bent upon finding out what manner of intruder lay in concealment there.

Facing the slight sounds Max waited, and watched, and listened. If his pulses were bounding much faster than their wont it was not surprising, for as yet he had not the slightest idea as to what might happen.

Should this, for instance, be one of the ferocious wild-cats for which the island had been famous long before Wesley Coombs ever dreamed of settling there, Max felt that he would hardly find himself in an enviable position; since the gloom under the trees must prevent him from seeing how to aim with certainty.

Given daylight, and that faithful little gun, the boy would not have thought it anything terrible to face at close quarters the biggest and most savage wild-cat ever known; for his charge of birdshot might be counted on to serve the purpose of a large bullet, and tear a hole in the side of the beast.

It was far different at dead of night, and such a dark night at that. And Max, while he could hardly be said to have had very much experience in that line, knew from hearing old Trapper Jim up in the North Woods tell stories that a wounded bobcat was one of the meanest things to run up against known to hunters.

The sounds kept on, and even became slightly plainer. This would surely indicate that the animal must be drawing nearer in his cautious way. Perhaps it was only curiosity that urged him on. Max hoped so from the bottom of his boyish heart. He did not have any desire to find a savage denizen of the wilds fastened on his back, clawing and tearing with the fury of a demon, while he himself would be almost helpless to get at his enemy.

Max was determined on one thing. No matter about the escaped convict and their desire to capture him, self-preservation must stand first on the calendar; and if he really found himself in a position where he anticipated an attack from the big cat, he meant to pour in the contents of both barrels, and then take chances.

As he continued to watch, always in the one quarter, where the slight noise indicated the presence of the creeping beast, Max saw something that riveted his attention immediately. At first he thought it was a glowworm, or possibly a firefly that had not yet arisen from the lush grass in which it lay concealed during the daytime.

Then, with a sudden shock, he realized what it was, for now there were two of the glowing spots, and close together. The cat had turned its head slightly, exposing both eyes. Like the orbs of all creatures of the feline species its eyes in the darkness glowed as though they were made of phosphorus.

It was far from a pleasant sight. Small wonder that the boy's hands trembled a little as he raised his gun, so as to cover those twin spots of yellow fire. He did not want to shoot, and only meant to do so as a very last resort; but since there was no telling what the treacherous brute might attempt to do, Max felt that he must keep himself in readiness every second of the time.

One thing brought him a little reassurance; so far as he could ascertain now, the bobcat was no longer advancing. Doubtless it lay there, stretched out upon a convenient log, and intently watching the crouching figure among the bushes, which it undoubtedly recognized as belonging to the hated, and also feared, human family.

Max stared as hard as he could straight back. He wanted it to understand that he was not in the least afraid, for that was what would count most when facing a wild beast.

A woman had been known to set a tiger in flight by opening her red parasol and rushing straight at him; while a bugler, about to be devoured by a lion, frightened the animal away by waving his arms and blowing all sorts of weird notes on his instrument.

Another man Max had heard of, upon finding himself at the mercy of a tiger, being utterly unarmed, was inspired to throw himself over, so that he stood upon his hands, waving both feet in the air, and in this posture advancing, finally dropping upon all fours, and still running toward the beast. Unable to understand what manner of creature this was the tiger slunk away.

For a space of perhaps five minutes, which to Max were like so many hours, the curious bobcat remained there, watching him as a cat might a mouse at play. Then the boy plainly heard the animal give a snarl as of utter disgust, and the glowing orbs vanished; while he could hear the pat of velvet-shod feet as they landed on another log.

At any rate, the beast had withdrawn, much to the relief of the lad. And again he was free to take up his own business of watching for the return of the occupant of the strange cabin on Catamount Island.

Another period of waiting, and Max again caught a slight sound. At first he feared that his former visitor, the bobcat, had returned with the intention of making a closer investigation; but, after listening, he became convinced that this was not the case.

Now it was a peculiar rustling among the dead leaves that lay under the trees, no fire having ever swept across the island, at least for many years. The sound was really continuous, and could hardly be made by the passage of any animal—mink, skunk, weasel, 'coon, 'possum or even muskrat.

Then it must be some sort of snake that was gliding along close by him. Again did the boy feel a sense of repulsion. He knew that it had long been said the island up the Big Sunflower was a nest of rattlesnakes, though so far none of them had seen even one of the scaly reptiles. What if this were one of the deadly species that was being attracted toward his crouching form?

He could not refrain from making some movement, with the intention of frightening it away; and was immediately gratified by hearing the slight rustling pass off to one side, as though his ruse had been successful.

This was really getting monotonous, and he found himself wondering when it might come to an end. What could be delaying the man? Had he, Max, miscalculated, so that the unknown party would not be apt to try to enter the camp until away toward morning? Or could it be that the boys were sitting up unusually late?

Max hardly believed this latter was the case, since he had asked them to retire shortly after he left; and supposed that they would heed his wishes in the matter, knowing how important it was to start things going.

So he finally concluded that the man himself was unduly cautious. Well, he had reason to be, if, as they now believed, he chanced to be an escaped prisoner, who had broken out from the penitentiary, and was trying to elude recapture by hiding in this remote and unusual haunt.

But surely it could not be much longer. Why, it seemed to Max that hours must have elapsed since he parted from his chums, and started on this little private enterprise of his own. Much had happened to him in that time, and he marveled to think how events could crowd upon each other's heels, once they started.

There was that little adventure with Ted Shafter and his followers, whereby he had, by a clever ruse, sent the fellows hurrying back down the river, and given them such a good scare that they would never again bother the campers on Catamount Island.

Then came the affair with the prowling bobcat; and Max would certainly not soon forget the chilly sensation that held possession of him all the time he could see those twin glowing yellow orbs fastened upon him.

And last, though far from least, had been that fear when he found reason to believe a passing rattler was within half a dozen feet of him.

Could there be any further danger to be met? He knew of none, and hoped nothing might occur to give him another thrill such as those that had passed. For while Max Hastings might be said to be a resolute lad, about as fearless as the ordinary boy of his years, perhaps more so, still he did not yearn for excitement.

There was Steve now, who was quite another proposition; he just dearly loved a racket, and was never so happy as when he felt that there was a fight of some sort in prospect, he cared very little what its nature.

How much longer could he stand it? And was midnight far past? Max would have given something for a chance to glance at the little nickel watch he carried; but the flash of a lighted match might come just at a time to ruin his carefully laid plans, and he declined to take the risk.

There was no striking clock in a church tower to tell him of the night, such as he was accustomed to at home; and Max was hardly woodsman enough to be able to read the stars and know by that means.

The thought came to him with great force, however, as he lay there looking up at the few stars he could see through the leafy canopy overhead; and Max determined that henceforth he would place himself in position to know just when certain bright stars might be expected to rise above the eastern horizon each succeeding night or others set in the west.

His long vigil was fated to come to an end at last, however. When the boy was almost ready to give up, and confess that sleep was mastering his desire to accomplish things, he heard a sound again.

Ah, this time it could be neither the rustle of a cat's body through the foliage nor the sinuous movements of a gliding snake along the ground. Closer it drew, and again did Max hold his breath with suspense; for now he knew beyond a doubt that a human being was approaching with hurried steps, and that the unknown headed toward the cabin, coming from down the island, too!

Once Max allowed himself to suspect that it might be one of his chums trying to find his place of concealment, and that something dreadful might have happened in camp that required his immediate presence. This thought, however, he immediately put aside as nonsense. It must be the inmate of the strange cabin who, having stolen the provisions, just as Max had expected he would, was now making a bee line for his retreat with the intention of devouring the same!

Closer came the rushing sound, as of the passage of some large form. Max had, it seemed, been wise to choose his hiding place in a thicket, where no one would think of going, for in this way he avoided contact with the stranger.

Directly past him Max saw a moving bulk go, and all he could make out was that the other was a man of unusual proportions, a giant in fact.

Then he heard him come up against the wall of the cabin, give a grunt, grope around for the door, and pass within.

After which the sound of the door closing came agreeably to the ears of the boy.

CHAPTER XIV.

HOW THE SCHEME WORKED.

"Now it's about time for me to be doing something!"

That was what Max whispered to himself, after he was sure the unknown party had taken up his quarters within that queer cabin with the green roof and lichen-covered walls.

The very thought of being able to move, and start doing things, seemed a relief. His muscles were so cramped from long sitting in the one position that at first he experienced quite severe twinges, when he started to leave the hiding place he had been occupying for some hours at least.

It took Max but a very short time to creep up to the side of the cabin. He had to be exceedingly careful, to be sure, since he could not tell what keen ears the fugitive from justice might possess. And surely an escaped convict would be apt to always be on the alert for sounds calculated to spell danger to him.

Before reaching the wall, however, Max had made a discovery. As is usual in the case of old log cabins that have stood neglected for many years, subject to storms, and the heat of summer, as well as the wintry blasts, some of the dried mud that had once been plastered between the logs to fill in the "chinks" had become loosened and fallen away.

Max had noted this fact before when prowling around. Indeed, ere entering the suspected cabin on that very day, he had taken the precaution to glue an eye to one of these cracks, and endeavor to find out whether it were safe for him to go in.

And now, through these same chinks there came streams of light, showing that the occupant possessed a supply of matches at least, and had lighted something that served him for a candle; possibly a long splinter of lightwood, picked up in the daytime at a point where the lightning had riven a resinous pine tree, and scattered it over the surrounding ground.

With the intention of seeing what the escaped convict looked like, Max made for one of these slender openings that ran the same way as the horizontal logs. He, of course, picked out the one that seemed to offer him the best advantages, in that it was a trifle larger than any of the rest.

Avoiding the shaft of light all he could, until ready to thrust his face up to the logs, and fill in the gap, Max crept along on hands and knees, trailing his gun.

He could hear slight movements from within, as though the man might be doing something. Max could give a pretty good guess what that was, if, as he suspected, the bait had been taken from the trap in the camp, and the convict arrived here with his arms filled with provisions.

Now Max was close enough to be able to accomplish the end he had in view. The very second he fastened his eye to that slender aperture he felt a thrill pass over his frame again, similar to that which had attacked him at the time he faced the crouching wild-cat.

He saw a man seated tailor fashion, with his legs crossed, on the hard earthen floor of the cabin. He seemed to be tearing at some food with almost the ferocity of a half-starved dog.

Max looked in vain for the expected and well-known stripes that would distinguish a prison convict. This man did not wear anything of the sort. His garments were of a very ordinary kind, though just now exceedingly ill kept, from groveling in the dirt, and sleeping night and day without taking them off.

His hair seemed to be rather long and unkempt, while there was a wild look in his face; and the way he cast his staring eyes about sent a cold chill into the heart of the watching lad.

Max realized that after all he and his chums had made a very poor guess of it, when they tried to figure things out. But he also felt a little satisfaction when he remembered how he had declared the footprint was made by a common shoe, such as inmates in all public institutions wore, as they are made in prisons by those who are serving long sentences.

This wretched man, then, was no escaped convict; but he was undoubtedly a crazy being, who, having fled from some retreat, thought to elude recapture by hiding in this lonely place!

Max hardly knew what to think. The change was so complete that he felt as though he must alter his plans in accordance with the new line-up. It would have been all right for the boys to help recapture a desperate criminal, whose being at large was a constant menace to the peaceful community; but would the same apply when it was a lunatic who kept house in that strange cabin on Catamount Island?

No matter what he decided, he must make his mind up quickly. The man looked very dangerous, though Max knew that appearances are very deceptive when those who are out of their right minds are concerned. Often the very man who seems most harmless is the crafty one ready to commit a terrible deed; while he who looks to be a veritable terror may turn out to be a mild fellow, who would not harm an ant.

Rapidly he ran things over in his mind. Why, evidently anyone devoid of sense and reason had no right to be at large. While he might manage to live through the summer, by snaring birds and catching fish, what would happen to the poor fellow when the biting blasts of bitter winter swept down from the cold Northland!

No matter who he was, where he came from, and what his object in hiding here might be, it were better that his presence be made known to the authorities. Somewhere or other they must be looking for him, since even the helpless inmates of public institutions for the insane are objects of concern; and one of them at large will create a reign of terror in a community, especially among the women.

"I must do it!" Max was saying to himself, as he continued to watch the wretched man tear away at the food, and act as though he were a wild beast rather than a human being, once gifted with a mind that could reason, love, hate, and learn.

As he had explained to his chums, when they pressed him, ere consenting that he venture upon this night expedition alone, Max had fixed it so that when the opportunity arrived he could fasten the door of the cabin securely.

A stout log would do the business. He had examined it, yes, and even tried the effect when he placed it in a leaning position against the door, although declining to go inside at the time, as he did not want to be caught in his own trap.

It had worked splendidly, too; and once it was fixed as he meant to have it, the lad felt positive that no single man, however powerful he might be, confined within the shack, could dislodge that barrier.

It would take him only a little time, a minute or two at the most, to lift that log, and place it just where he wanted to have it. And Max was again pleased because he had gone through all the operation when there in daylight, since it made things so much easier now.

So he quitted his post at the open chink, where the light filtered through, and which had served his purpose so well in the line of observation.

It was to be hoped, in carrying out the balance of his scheme, he would not make any sound that, reaching the ears of that wild-looking inmate of the cabin, would bring him flying through the doorway. Max had not the slightest desire to come into close connection with the mysterious unknown crazy man. And his motives in attempting the capture of the other were purely along the line of kindness. If a man is unable to look after himself, then it stands to reason that he ought to have attention from those whom the state appoints as his guardians.

The log was where he had left it. Max knew this, for he had made it a point to feel for it at the time he crept close to the cabin, and listened for sounds of any sleeper being within.

He had to lay his gun aside, if he wished to work out his plan, for he must use both arms, and every pound of muscle he could summon to the fore, such was the heaviness of the log.

It was a minute of considerable suspense while Max was carrying that log forward.

He reached the door, and nothing had happened, thank goodness. And it was with a grateful heart that the boy presently carefully planted the log in the position he had fixed upon as being best.

Now one end rested against the door, which opened outwardly by good luck; while the other dug into the ground, and was held by the end of a huge rock that cropped up close to the surface just in that convenient spot.

Max drew the first decent breath he had had since starting to carry out his daring project. He believed that he had the trap so arranged now that escape from it was well-nigh impossible; and yet almost immediately his heart seemed to jump in his throat with sudden apprehension.

Perhaps in dropping the log into place he may have made some little sound that reached the ears of the crazy man within the cabin. Max heard a shuffling of feet. Then the door was shaken, at first gently, and then with more and more violence, until the very walls of the cabin seemed to quiver under the force employed.

Although he had been so very confident before, Max now experienced a new feeling of acute alarm. What if the imprisoned man succeeded in breaking out of his place of confinement, would he not be raging mad in every sense of the word, and in a humor to attack the camp of the boy chums?

Max had started to grope for his gun, but as this fear sprang into being again, instead of doing that he stumbled over to where he knew of a second log lying on the ground; perhaps where poor Wesley Coombs had left it in that long ago time, when he started to make a home in this wild land.

Frantically Max tugged at this larger log. Under ordinary circumstances he might not have been able to have more than moved the heavy tree trunk; but keyed up to a pitch of desperation by the conditions that confronted him, he bent himself to the task with a strength equal to that of almost any man.

Rolling the log along until he had brought it to just the proper point where it could be best used, Max exerted himself once more, and to some purpose. Afterwards he wondered himself how he had ever accomplished such a feat, because it did look far beyond the power of a half-grown lad. But necessity compels all of us to do things that, in our calmer moments, we would call preposterous, and out of reason.

All Max knew was that the log went up against the door, that was quivering under the attacks of the crazy man within.

He drew a sigh of relief when assured of this fact. Panting for breath he stood there and listened. The walls and roof he knew were absolutely sound, which had seemed wonderful enough, considering all the years that the cabin had stood here unoccupied.

It would take any man hours to dig under those logs, and burrow out, especially if he had no hatchet or knife to assist in the labor, as Max believed was the case now. And long before that happened he could have his four chums on the spot, ready to lend the assistance of their strong young arms in securing the escaping prisoner.

What they should do about it, Max as yet hardly knew. This was a matter in which he felt he would like to have the advice of grave and thoughtful Owen. Four of them might keep guard over the raging madman, trying to appease him by thrusting bits of tempting food through the cracks; while the fifth fellow sped down the river in one of the canoes to bring help from Carson.

And right then and there Max was boy enough to feel that it would be something of a feather in their caps if, in addition to camping a whole week on Catamount Island, they could lay the ghost that had frightened Herb and his friends at the time they tried to spend a single night in the strange cabin.

But he must not waste any more time here. Minutes were worth something, with the trap sprung, and a desperate lunatic caught.

He must hasten back to the camp, tell his chums all that had happened, and after arming them as best could be done, they must hurry to the cabin. Max had decided that Owen ought to be the one to spin down the Big Sunflower as soon as the first peep of daylight appeared in the east. He would not dare allow him to attempt the voyage in the dense darkness, for fear of a spill, and possible peril; since there were many cross currents, and rocks that would sink a frail canoe if struck at full speed.

Now the man seemed to have become quiet again. Max hoped that he had realized the foolishness of trying to break through the door, and that the lure of the stolen food had drawn him back to his feast. He listened, and could catch just the faintest of sounds, which it was impossible to analyze. But above all else the anxious boy hoped that his captive might not think about burrowing under the log wall, at least not for some time yet.

And so, having finally located his gun again, Max turned away from the cabin, meaning to retrace his course along the shore to the camp where his chums would be found.

CHAPTER XV.

UNEXPECTED ALLIES.

It was with a feeling of thankfulness, as well as a sense of satisfaction, that Max Hastings started to head for the shore of the island once more. By this time he felt that he ought to know every foot of the way, after passing over it so often. And it afforded an easier passage than by keeping straight through the dense underbrush and woods; though the crazy man seemed to prefer that course, having a possible secret trail of his own.

As the island was not many acres in extent, Max expected to reach the camp before ten minutes had elapsed, or fifteen at most. The boys would be anxious to see him. Perhaps they had been sitting up inside the tents all the time, too worried to go to sleep. If so, he wondered whether they had known when the wild man of the woods again entered the camp, and made way with the provisions waiting for him.

Reaching the shore, where he could look out upon the passing river, he turned his head in the quarter whence he knew his destination lay.

In this way then he had been going, perhaps five minutes, and all seemed well, when he met with a sudden and disagreeable surprise.

Something sprang upon him without the least warning. Max, although horrified, and with that ferocious bobcat in mind, attempted to struggle the best he knew how; but to his astonishment his arms were pinioned at his sides, so that he really found himself helpless to move, as he was thrown heavily down.

Of course he had understood before this that it was not an animal at all that had jumped upon him, but a human being like himself. His first thought lay in the direction of the madman whom he had left in the cabin with the barricaded door. In some mysterious way the

110

fellow must have escaped, and following fast upon his heel had now accomplished his capture.

And just when this awful thought was getting a grip on the mind of poor Max, he found occasion to change his opinion once more. A face had come in contact with his, and it was smooth, and destitute of the hair he had seen straggling over the long unshaven countenance of the crazy man.

Could Ted Shafter and his cronies have dared venture back after receiving that severe fright earlier in the evening? The idea seemed next door to preposterous to Max; but what other explanation could there be to the mystery.

"Got him safe, Jenkins?" asked a gruff voice close by; and Max realized that it was a question addressed to the unseen party who held him so tightly.

"That's what I have, sir; but seems to me there's something wrong here," replied the other party, the athletic fellow to whom Max owed his tumble.

"What d'ye mean by saying that, Jenkins?" demanded the man who seemed to be in authority, since the second one called him "sir," and seemed ready to obey his orders.

"He don't feel near as big as our man; and his face, it's as smooth as my own. I reckon we've hit on the wrong bird, Mr. Lawrence," continued the man, slightly relaxing his firm grip on Max.

"I'm sure you have," said the boy, thinking that it was time he let these mysterious parties know that he seriously objected to being set upon, pulled down, and roughly treated, just as though he were a common criminal.

"Well, this *is* a joke on us, sure enough," remarked the man who gave orders; "let him up, Jenkins; it must be one of the boys we saw through the glasses yesterday camped at the foot of the island. They didn't go back home after all, as we believed, when we came back here with a boat this evening. That must have been another lot we heard coming down the river."

Max began to grasp things now. From these words he knew that these two men must be the same whom Steve had seen watching the island on the day before, and who had appeared to go away *up* the river. They must have circled around, so as to finally reach Carson, where they heard certain things that had sent them up again, this time in a boat, late the afternoon before.

And hearing the splash of oars as Ted and his cronies hurried back to town, they had believed that the boys were those whom they had seen camped at the lower end of the island. Doubtless they even suspected that Max and his chums might have been also frightened off by the same wild-looking man who had appeared to Herb Benson weeks ago.

"Who are you, and what are you looking for over here on Catamount Island?" Max now asked, boldly, feeling pretty sure he could give a good guess, even before the other spoke a word in explanation.

The crackle of a match told him that the leader of the couple wished to take a look at him, so as to be satisfied. And when the little piece of wood flared up, Max was able to see that both men were, as Steve had declared, dressed in gray uniforms, that were decorated with the brass buttons of authority.

"Well, it *is* a boy, as sure as anything, Jenkins," remarked the man, who wore a short-pointed beard, and had a keen face, as though he might be in the habit of dealing with charges who required constant vigilance. "Now, I hope my assistant didn't hurt you much when he jumped you, following my orders, when he heard you coming?"

Now, Max did feel a trifle sore, where he had struck the ground with the said Jenkins on top of him; and doubtless the feeling would be still more pronounced by another day. But then he was too proud to confess to any such small thing.

"Nothing to mention, sir," he remarked, just as though it were a common thing to have people wallow all over him, as though they were playing tackle in a football struggle. "But are you looking for a lunatic?"

"Hello! Do you mean to say you can put us on the track of one?" demanded the man who had been called Mr. Lawrence by his assistant.

"A rather big man, with a shock of white hair, and staring eyes; a man dressed in a faded suit of brown, and wearing an old blue flannel shirt?" Max went on.

He could not see the men now, because the match had long since gone out; but it was evident that they were delighted to hear him talk in the way he did.

"You've described him to a dot, my lad," remarked the gentleman; "only his hair was cut fairly short, and his face smooth, when he broke loose from the asylum, now two months back, and disappeared. Such a job I never before struck. We've been on twenty different trails, and everyone turned out false. And we were about to give it up, when I remembered that long ago he had lived in this section of the country; and the idea came to me that perhaps even a crazy man might remember places. So we came up here to look at the island, only to find a party of boys camped on it; and that seemed to indicate a crazy man could not be anywhere near them. But down in Carson I heard a story from a boy about a wild-looking creature that had frightened himself and his friends nearly to death up here on the island; so, not knowing what else to do, Jenkins and myself got a boat and came back, meaning to explore the place in the night time, as well as by daylight. We intended going back home and giving it all up as a bad job, if this last hope failed, and we didn't locate old Coombs in the place he once lived, they told me."

Max uttered a cry.

"What was that name you spoke, sir?" he asked.

"Why, the name of the lunatic that broke out, and has given us all this chase over the blessed country; Wesley Coombs his full name is. Have you heard of him, my boy?" replied the warden of the asylum.

"Oh, yes, and to think that when he escaped, after being confined for so many years, the poor man turned back here to the last place he had lived when he had a wife and child. They were both drowned in a freshet. I understood he had gone, too; but he must have been taken to the lunatic asylum instead, poor fellow."

Max was feeling very sad as the truth broke in upon him after this fashion. To think that Wesley Coombs had been alive all these years; restrained of his liberty. And how pathetic it was to know that when he finally found an opportunity to get away, he had, through some queer freak of fate, come back to this island of the Big Sunflower, where he had brought his young wife and child years ago, and which still remained, the one remembrance of the past in his poor dulled mind!

"Is he here now on the island?" asked Mr. Lawrence, eagerly.

Perhaps Wesley Coombs was a person of very little importance in himself; but he had been sought for so long that his recapture would bring considerable satisfaction along with it.

"To the best of my knowledge and belief, he is," replied Max, chuckling to think how he was in a condition to know, and enjoying the prospect of springing a surprise upon the two wardens of the asylum.

"Then you've seen him?" continued the head keeper.

"I certainly have, sir, or I couldn't have described him very well," Max went on, not too anxious to make his disclosure; for he thought he ought to enjoy the situation a little, after experiencing that rough tumble.

"Can you take us to where we can find him?" next asked the warden.

"Inside of five minutes, sir. I was just on the way to get the rest of my chums, and then send for assistance, because I've caught the crazy man in a trap!"

"A trap! D'ye hear that, Jenkins? This lad has been able to do what you and I would have given a lot to accomplish. What sort of a trap, would you mind telling us, young man?" continued Mr. Lawrence, with more respect in his voice than at any time previous.

"In his old log cabin, sir," Max replied, "where once upon a time he used to live. He has been sleeping there every night, but hiding in the thick jungle during the day. Several times now he's gone and raided our camp for provisions, which he would take to the cabin, and eat up. So I fixed it for him to get something more to-night, while I waited up here, ready to fasten the door of the cabin with a log."

"Well, that sounds clever of you, I must say," remarked the other, admiration in his voice, "and the trap worked, did it?"

"He came along, and he walked into the cabin. Somehow he must have secured a supply of matches, for he has been having fires there, sir; and he lighted a splinter of wood when he came in to-night. I peeped through a chink and saw him for the first time. He gave me a chill, I tell you. You see, we got the idea in our heads that it was an escaped convict hiding out on the island; but none of us ever thought of a crazy man, and poor old Wesley Coombs at that."

"After he went in you fastened the door, did you?" the other asked.

"I had a heavy log handy, and this I propped up against the door, so no single man could ever push it open. But because he threw himself against it so hard I dragged a second one over to back up the first. And now, sir, I'm sure he can't get out of that cabin unless he takes to burrowing under the logs; which would take him hours; for he had no knife, and the earth is as hard as stone there."

"Well done, my lad. Allow me to thank you for the great help you have given us, and to congratulate you as well. Shake hands, won't you, please," and this Max did with all the sincerity in the world.

"And I sure hope you don't hold any grudge against me, young feller, because I bumped your head when I took you in?" remarked Jenkins, as he, too, brushed up, and felt for the hand of the boy in the darkness.

"Why, of course not," replied Max, giving an unseen grimace as his bruised side hurt him just then. "You were only doing what you thought was your duty; and, after seeing that wild man, I can understand that he must be strong as an ox, and I suppose violent, too."

"Oh, no, not a bit," declared Mr. Lawrence; "that is, he's never been so in the past. No keeper ever had the least trouble with old Coombs. They all liked him, because he was so gentle and tractable. But would you mind taking us to that cabin now, young fellow!"

"I wish you'd go with me down to our camp first," said Max.

"To be sure we will, and it's a very little favor to ask after doing us such a good turn; but what's the idea, my boy?" asked the head warden, cheerfully.

"My name is Max Hastings," replied the boy, who did not just fancy being called "my boy" and "young fellow" any too much. "You see, I wanted to have my four chums on hand at the time you opened the door, and secured poor old Wesley Coombs. We can get back there in a jiffy, and they'd be ever so much obliged for the chance of seeing how the last thing worked."

"Well, it seems to be your game all along, Max, since we don't even know where this strange old cabin, that we've been hearing so much about lately, is located. So, as you promise to lead us back there with as little delay as possible, certainly we'll go with you. And the sooner we start, the quicker we can be back again."

That was a hint from Mr. Lawrence that Max could not ignore. There was logic and a world of truth back of it, too.

"Come on then, please, sir; the going is better close to the shore line; and that's the way I came up."

With that he started, the others trailing along in his wake. And Max chuckled to himself more than a few times while thus drawing nearer and nearer to the camp, where a great surprise awaited his chums.

CHAPTER XVI.

THE LAST CAMP FIRE ON CATAMOUNT ISLAND.

"Hello! In camp, there, ahoy! Show a head!"

That was the way Max shouted, as he broke into the circle of light cast by the camp fire, none too good just then, on account of lack of attention.

Instantly several heads appeared in view, two at each tent flap, to be exact.

"It's Max, all right!" shouted Steve.

"And, say, what's this he's gone and brought back with him, fellers?" cried Bandy-legs, staring in surprise at the two men, with their gray uniforms and brass buttons of authority.

The four boys now came creeping forth. And when he saw that all of them were fully dressed, Max knew that sleep could hardly have visited the camp during his long absence.

"These are my chums, gentlemen," remarked Max, as he bent a smiling face on the staring quartette. "The one on the right is my cousin, Owen Hastings; next to him comes Toby Jucklin; then this boy is Bandy-legs Griffin, who is much better than he looks; and the last of all is Steve Dowdy, or 'Touch-and-go Steve' we call him. And this gentleman is Mr. Lawrence, while his assistant is Jenkins."

"From the penitentiary, of course; I can see the uniform?" remarked Steve.

"Wrong again, old fellow," laughed Max. "They happen to be wardens from the State Asylum for the Insane!"

118

"What?" gasped Steve. "Ain't they looking for a desperate escaped jail bird?"

"Not at all, but an escaped lunatic; a man who got away some months back, and has kept hidden ever since here on this island, while they've been searching all over for him. And, fellows, you'll be surprised as much as I was when you hear who the poor chap really is we've been feeding with our ham and other grub. Steve, remember what you heard your father say about the man who once started to make his home on Catamount Island; but the flood came and upset his plans?"

"Say, do you mean Wesley Coombs?" demanded Steve, quickly.

"Yes," replied Max. "Well, you got things a little mixed there. He lost his wife and baby in the freshet, but he was saved, though his mind was always a blank; and all these years the poor fellow has been shut up in the lunatic asylum. He managed to escape a while ago, and seems to have been drawn back here to the place where he was last happy. And now they've come after him to take him back, for he'd he frozen to death, or starve, if left loose here winter times."

"But can they get him, d'ye think?" asked Steve.

"Oh, that's dead easy for them," returned the other, trying to keep from displaying anything like pride in his voice or manner. "You see I've got him shut up in the old cabin right now. We only came down here to get you fellows, and then these gentlemen want to hike back there to make the capture."

"Whoop! It takes Max to do big things!" shouted Steve.

"He never bites off more'n he can chaw!" asserted Bandy-legs, appearing to be supremely happy over the improved prospect of things.

"I'm rather inclined to agree with you, boys," remarked the head warden. "Max has certainly done himself proud on this special occasion; and we're placed under a heavy debt of gratitude to him. But if you're ready, boys, we might as well make a start. The sooner we have our man in custody, the easier we'll feel. He's given us such a long chase that it'll be good to know we can bring him back to his old quarters, where he seemed fully contented until the chance came to skip. None of 'em can ever let that pass by, no matter how satisfied they are. It's a part of the disease, the doctors tell us."

So they started forth, taking both lanterns with them so that they might have plenty of light along the way. Not one of the boys felt the slightest alarm about leaving the camp unprotected now; especially after Max had described how he gave Ted Shafter and his cronies such a good scare.

"We saw the flash, Max," remarked Owen, "just when we were thinking of getting under cover, like you suggested. And we heard the yells, too. All of us thought we recognized the voice of Ted, and we had a pretty good guess coming that you'd given 'em something to remember."

"Say," remarked Steve, laughingly, "when they went shooting past the lower end of the island as fast as they could row, they were chattering like a lot of old crows. We kept as mum as oysters, and let the lot go. It was a good riddance of bad rubbish anyhow, and we didn't want to hold 'em back for one minute."

The return journey was easily accomplished, with Max to lead the way, swinging one of the lighted lanterns in his hand.

As they left the shore and headed in toward the place where the old cabin stood, all of them were listening to ascertain whether the inmate were beating against the fast door, and perhaps shrieking as only a madman might.

But all seemed very quiet.

"Chances are he's digging a tunnel under the wall, like you said he might, Max," suggested Steve.

"Well, he's in there safe and sound, anyhow," replied Max, in a satisfied tone.

After reaching the cabin the head warden went up to the door, and, with the help of the others, threw both logs down.

"Hello, in there, Wesley Coombs, this is Warden Lawrence, come to take you back to your comfortable quarters at the palace."

With that he threw open the door, and lantern in hand stalked in. The wild man was sitting there on the hard earthen floor, and engaged in calmly eating. He merely glanced up as they entered, and paid no further attention to them, which rather pleased Max, for he had feared a terrible struggle, and secretly deep down in his heart felt a great pity for poor old Wesley Coombs.

The crazy man seemed to recognize the badge of authority in the uniforms of the two wardens, for he obeyed their slightest orders without the least hesitation. But Max was pleased to see that there did not seem to be cringing fear in connection with this obedience, such as would rather indicate that he might have been badly used at times in the past by men wearing these same uniforms.

They all went back to the camp; and since sleep seemed next to impossible, after such exciting times, they just sat around talking. The two wardens proved very pleasant fellows indeed; and declared that the cup of coffee which was brewed for them was nectar, "ambrosia," Mr. Lawrence called it.

When morning came the wardens took their prisoner away. Poor Wesley Coombs seemed to cast one last pitiful glance back at the island ere he passed from the sight of the youthful campers. No doubt he was safely returned to the asylum; for some time later Max received a very courteous letter from the superintendent in charge of the institution, thanking him and his friends very warmly for the aid they had given the wardens in effecting the recapture of the escaped lunatic, But it would always give Max a queer little feeling of pain deep down in the region of his heart every time he thought of the wild man of Catamount Island, and what a sad memory of the dim past it had been that drew him back there after so many years of blankness had ensued.

Now the balance of their stay on the island partook more of the nature of a picnic than anything else. With the passing of the supposed "ghost" of the strange cabin, there no longer remained anything to disturb their peace of mind. Ted Shafter and his crowd would certainly give the place a wide berth from that time out; and with reasonable precaution the boys need not fear contact with any wild-cat or poisonous snake while staying there.

On the last morning of their camping experience, while they were beginning to dismantle the tents, and prepare for loading the canoes, quite a flotilla hove in sight down the river, there being three boats, each rowed by a couple of weary boys.

It turned out to be Herb Benson and some of his friends, who had started from Carson very early in the morning, and had just been able to make the island before noon. Of course it was mostly curiosity to see whether Max and his chums had really spent the whole week on the island that had brought them up.

But enough provisions remained to give the entire crowd a dinner; and feeling refreshed after this, they were ready to start back with the current, a much easier task than butting against it.

Sitting there, and enjoying the hospitality of the five campers, Herb and his friends listened to an account of the many things that had happened. And how their eyes did distend with wonder and interest when they heard all about the wild man of the strange cabin of the island, whose sudden appearance at the time the others occupied that shack had driven them away in mad haste.

They frankly admitted that Max and the rest possessed more grit than they had given them credit for, and that the little wager had been decided in their favor. After all, our five boys had enjoyed the outing more than words could tell; and were then, one and all declared, ready to repeat the experience at the earliest possible opportunity.

That time was closer at hand than any of them suspected when speaking of their desire to again get together under cover of the tents.

They made the return trip in pretty fast time, the canoes gliding along as if drawn by unseen hands, as the paddles flashed in the light of the westering sun. It had been a week of many surprises, and not a few thrills, that would haunt them for a long time to come. And among all the other things for which they believed they had reason to be thankful, that little episode in connection with the Shafter crowd stood out prominently. No doubt, in time, the fellows would learn what it was that had given them such a grand scare; and they would also try to make out that they guessed it all along, and had only fled because their presence had become known; but Max would only smile if he heard that. He would never forget the cries of genuine alarm that had gone up from that boat, when the awful glare suddenly burst out from the bushes of the haunted island.

Of course, one of the first things done after reaching town was to hand the cedar canoe over to the local boat builder, and have him put a new garboard streak in the bottom, to take the place of the defective one, which had been bored through and then artfully plugged, in such a way that it would not be noticed, yet must work loose at some time perhaps when far up the river, as we know it did.

They never really found out just who was guilty of such a mean act; but felt positive that it could originate in no other brain but that of Ted Shafter, even if actually committed by his shadow, Shack Beggs.

The boathouse was soon improved, and made so strong that the boys felt they could defy such conspirators; for they hardly believed Ted was ready to set fire to a building, and take the chances of being sent away to a reform school, in order to get square with some of those boys he hated bitterly.

That his enmity would endure, and give Max and his chums further cause for anxiety, all those who knew the stubborn nature of the Carson bully felt convinced.

What befell the five chums on another outing trip which soon followed the camp on Catamount Island, with many thrilling adventures, and a mystery in the bargain, will be found recorded in the pages of the next story in the "Camp Fire and Trail Series," entitled "Lost in the Great Dismal Swamp."

9 781406 559156